Side Trips

*To Sandy —
with best wishes,*

[signature]

Side Trips

by

Gavin R. Dobson

Librario

Published by

Librario Publishing Ltd.

ISBN 13: 978-1906775-094

Copies can be ordered via the Internet
www.librario.com

or from:

Brough House, Milton Brodie, Kinloss
Moray IV36 2UA
Tel/Fax No 00 44 (0)1343 850 617

Printed and bound in the UK by
4edge Ltd, Hockley. www.4edge.co.uk

Typeset by 3btype.com

© Gavin R. Dobson

The Author has asserted his moral right to be identified as the author of this work. This book or any part of it may not be reproduced without permission from the author.

Contents

Foreword		7
Chapter 1	A Day in New Zealand	9
Chapter 2	Chicago Burns	25
Chapter 3	The Shard of Pottery	39
Chapter 4	Poisonous Old Git	53
Chapter 5	Café de la Paix	59
Chapter 6	San Andreas	71
Chapter 7	Gabbot's Meadow	89
Chapter 8	The Great Experiment	103
Chapter 9	Moving from New York	115
Chapter 10	The Literary Society	127
Chapter 11	Niki's Love	141
Chapter 12	The Swallow	153

Foreword

Thank you for picking up Side Trips.

This is the third volume of fiction short stories describing the adventures of Geordie Kinloch. They take place all over the globe as he snatches time away from business life and gets involved in a variety of escapades. I hope you enjoy reading them.

I dedicate this book to my mother. She passed away one Saturday last April as the daffodils blew wild in the Angus glens.

I dedicate this book to my father. He died a month later on a warm Kentish evening, to the scent of lilac and the buzz of insects in the chestnut trees.

Thank you for the wonderful life you gave us.

Logie, March 2009

Chapter 1

A Day in New Zealand

When he was a young merchant banker Geordie Kinloch flew first class and grew accustomed to resting his head on some of the world's most expensive pillows. He became quite at home at The George V in Paris, The Okura in Tokyo and The Oriental in Bangkok. He played golf at the Greenbriar and cut deals at the Negresco. As he jetted from city to city in pursuit of deals, however, he was always too preoccupied to explore the many pleasures his destinations had to offer.

A particularly tortuous contract was finally concluded after thirty hours of haggling, negotiating, eyeballing, posturing and threatening in a gilded suite in the Hotel d'Angleterre in Copenhagen. Geordie looked forward to returning to the office as the conquering hero, bearing a signed deal that would yield his employers £10m of fees in two years. After a rough night he flew home to London on the earliest flight, shaved, showered, changed into fresh clothes and ordered a taxi to take him to the offices of Kornfeld Neuhoffer in Bishopsgate.

He tapped on old Ephraim Neuhoffer's door. It was always open. "Yes, my boy. What can I do for you?" the octogenarian enquired.

"Just to let you know that we won the Offshore Danske Phase II contract. We were in stiff competition with Weinbergers but managed to pull it off after considerable negotiating. For a while I thought we'd lost it but Wakehurst and I trumped the deal by finessing the Sinking Fund and tightening terms on the Swap," Geordie announced breathlessly.

Ephraim Neuhoffer listened with a paternal smile. His elbows rested on the polished surface of his desk, hands finger-tip to finger-tip, church-style. His hair was thick, closely cropped and as black as tar, more characteristic of a 30-year-old than a man 20 years beyond normal retirement age. After Geordie finished gushing about his financial triumph in Copenhagen, Neuhoffer asked gently, "Did you see the Glyptotek?"

Geordie's face clouded. Had he missed a key clause, the absence of which would make the deal unravel and lock Kornfeld Neuhoffer into losses for years? How could he not have seen the Glyptotek?

"I'm sorry?"

"The Glyptotek," Neuhoffer repeated. He gave no clues. The young man was on the spot.

"I'll need to check with Wakehurst. I thought we had it covered. Can I get back to you about the Glyptotek later this morning?"

"I fear you wasted your trip to Copenhagen, Kinloch. But yes, please do get back to me later this morning."

Flustered and deflated, Geordie retreated from the infernally smiling old man, raced upstairs to the Corporate Finance department and burst into Wakehurst's office. Five Japanese gentlemen sat around him in a semicircle. They looked utterly blank, but attentive in a Japanese way. Wakehurst was droning about the absence of covenants in the small print of offshore bond prospectuses. He may as well have been trying to explain nuclear physics to a bunch of New Guinea Highlanders.

Affecting an air of calm urgency, Geordie broke in. "Sorry to disturb you, gentlemen, but I need a quick word with Mr Wakehurst."

Wakehurst glowered. "Please excuse me, gentlemen." Out in the corridor he turned on Geordie. "This'd bloody well better be important. I've got the Treasury team from Sumihui Bank in my office. I was about to close a Eurobond deal when you interrupted. What is it?"

"Did we remember the Glyptotek in the Danish deal?"

"Sorry?"

"The Glyptotek."

"What about it?"

"Did we remember it in the Danish deal?"

"What the hell are you talking about? The Glyptotek's a museum."

"I was talking to Old Man Neuhoffer about our deal and he asked if we'd seen the Glyptotek."

"The NY Carlsberg Glyptotek is arguably the greatest sculpture museum in the world. That's why he asked you. You were in Copenhagen: did you see the Glyptotek? You were in Paris: did you see the Eiffel Tower?" Noting Geordie's embarrassment, he turned to get back to his meeting, adding, "Bloody fool."

Geordie locked himself in a lavatory for 15 minutes to compose himself. After revealing his ignorance twice in quick succession he concluded that the best solution was to square up to it.

He tapped on Ephraim Neuhoffer's door.

"Yes, my boy. What can I do for you?"

"I'm afraid I've been rather stupid. When you asked about the Glyptotek . . ."

"You thought I was referring to an obscure but critical clause in your financing contract."

"I'm afraid so."

"Kinloch, you are the best rainmaker in our bank. How many times do you expect to live your life?"

"Er . . . Once."

"Precisely – then *live* it, Kinloch. My father always said that he expected me to explore the wonders of the world when I travelled on business. When I returned from trips he always asked what I had seen. What's the point of visiting wonderful cities and not tasting their fruits, Kinloch? You could easily have excused yourself for an hour when you were in Copenhagen. Even better, you might have adjourned the meeting, strolled round to the Glyptotek with your lawyers and enjoyed an excellent lunch in the café there. If you'd brought your potential clients along you might even have closed the deal sooner."

"I suppose I don't want to appear frivolous."

"Frivolous? Ach, man! There is no rule of business that says you can't use a bit of imagination and frivolity, Kinloch. Why sit on your backside all day when you can accomplish the same goal with a bit of excitement? Let me tell you about the Glyptotek . . ."

Without waiting for Geordie's reply, Neuhoffer waxed forth.

"In Greek a bibliotek is a collection of books, a pinakotek is a collection of paintings and a glyptotek is a collection of sculptures — a sculpture museum, Kinloch. A hundred years ago Carl Jacobsen made his fortune by brewing Carlsberg beer. He endowed the Glyptotek in the heart of Copenhagen. You can stand in awe before contemporary busts of great emperors like Augustus and Marcus Aurelius, look at Caligula's face oozing spite and weakness. Did you know it was a capital offence to look down on Caligula's head from above? Romans were forbidden to see he was bald. Gods don't go bald, do they, Kinloch?"

"Good question."

"Have you any idea what these fragments of marble have seen since they were carved? You stand alone in a room before a bust that might have been touched by the Emperor Hadrian himself. Can you conceive the power of that moment, Kinloch?"

"I can see your point, Mr Neuhoffer, but I would hate the bank to think I was on a jaunt when I was on a business trip."

"A jaunt, Kinloch? Stand quietly in front of a 1st century bust of Pompey for 10 minutes, study his powerful head, his bulbous nose, his virile crop of hair. This man ruthlessly wielded massive power 2000 years ago. The statue exudes it. When you return to the street it inspires you to win at business. Is that a jaunt?"

Before Geordie could respond, Neuhoffer continued. "My father expected his bankers to be civilized. Civilization is not about holding your knife and fork correctly and dabbing the corner of your mouth with a napkin, Kinloch. Civilized means that you have a profound sense of the well-spring of life, of the events in history that lead to this very moment. It's not your right to walk safely in the streets of London, Kinloch. It's your privilege."

Geordie sat silently, absorbing a lesson that no Ivy League MBA curriculum could possibly have taught.

"You can go now, Kinloch."

At lunchtime that day Geordie went for a walk in the April sunshine. He strolled across the Thames on Tower Bridge and listened to a Bach organ recital in Southwark Cathedral. His career had begun.

One evening the following September he was resting on his hotel bed after a frantic week of meetings around Australia. Scrolling through his emails, he spotted a staff release from the bank:

> The Directors of Kornfeld Neuhoffer regret to announce that chairman emeritus Ephraim Neuhoffer died of a ruptured aneurism last night while attending a private view of sculptures at a gallery in Bond Street. He will be sorely missed. Ephraim no longer held an active executive role at the bank so his position will not require to be replaced.

Geordie opened the balcony window and leaned on the railings, staring at the fading dusk over Sydney Harbour. The navigation lights of myriads of small boats shimmered on the darkening water like fireflies. The curiously lavatorial sounds of a didgeridoo, played by an itinerant aborigine far below, floated up with other street sounds. "What a hell of a loss," he said out loud. "Ephraim was the last civilized banker in the City of London."

He reflected on their last conversation a few months earlier. Geordie manifestly delivered great value to the bank; he had repaid their decision to hire him a thousand times over. He'd earned the privilege to enjoy himself while abroad on company business, but it simply wasn't his nature to take time off and goof around.

It was a Thursday evening. He had to be in Los Angeles by noon the following Wednesday. He'd planned to return to London the next day, change his shirts, pop into the bank on Sunday, get some paperwork out of the way, work all day Monday and fly to LA on Tuesday.

"Kinloch, you may never be in Australia again. Remember what I told you about the Glyptotek?" Neuhoffer's spirit whispered, "What have you seen of Australia but the inside of meeting rooms, taxis, planes and hotel suites?"

Geordie changed into casual clothes and strolled from his hotel in the Rocks across to the Royal Botanical Gardens. Closed at dusk. He made his way to the Art Gallery of New South Wales. It was reputed to contain a fabulous collection of works by Arthur Streeton. Closed. He turned inland towards the Central Business District. The streets were deserted. Disconsolately he headed back to his hotel.

In the window of a travel agency he spotted a large-scale map of the world. As he studied it he realized it was plainly idiotic to fly from Sydney to London to Los Angeles. It was half the distance just to cross the Pacific and fly straight to Los Angeles from Sydney.

Overnight he cancelled his return trip to London and emailed his colleagues to inform them he'd be flying directly to Los Angeles. After breakfast he returned to the travel agency he had passed the previous evening and stood at the desk of a blond, tanned young man.

"I've got five days to get to LA. What's worth seeing between here and there?"

"Pardon me?"

A DAY IN NEW ZEALAND

"It's Friday morning in Sydney and I need to be in Los Angeles by noon next Wednesday. I want an imaginative itinerary, a bit of island-hopping, some fun places to visit. Any ideas?"

"You having me on, mite?"

"Deadly serious."

"What's your budget?"

"Whatever it takes."

"How well do you know the South Pacific?"

"Not at all. Everything's new."

"When do you want to start?"

"Tonight."

"Been to New Zealand?"

"Never."

"Good. My name's Mike. I'll see if I can get you on a flight to Auckland tonight. Where do you want to go next?" The travel agent unfolded a map of the South Pacific in front of Geordie. "Depending on the availability of flights I'd recommend one of two routes. You can fly Auckland to Fiji to Hawaii and LA. Or you can fly Auckland to Papeete to LA. If you had more time we could look at side trips to Tonga and Samoa, but I think we should keep you on a straight line heading towards Los Angeles."

"That makes sense."

Half an hour passed, accompanied by the furious clacking of Mike's keyboard. Mike concocted an itinerary that would surely have made Ephraim Neuhoffer proud of him. It put Geordie for one day in New Zealand and two-and-a-half days in Tahiti. He would arrive in Los Angeles at 6 a.m. on Wednesday morning. Enough time to check into his hotel, take a swim, nap for three hours and attend his luncheon presentation before heading back to London the same afternoon.

Geordie boarded the aircraft for the night flight to Auckland. The universal protocol among first-class long-haul passengers is to keep to yourself. Geordie looked forward to cocooning himself in a deep reclining seat with a book and a light dinner. He liked to dream his dreams and think his thoughts alone, as did all experienced first-class travellers of his acquaintance.

He had just turned the fourth page of his book when a hand was thrust into his face. "Evening, mite. Name's Cedric Sedgwick. Friends call me Ced. Going to Auckland, then, are you?" Geordie looked up and saw a tall ruddy-faced Australian taking the seat beside him.

"Well, yes. That's the general intention." Geordie kept his finger pointedly on the line he was reading, sending a clear 'Do not disturb' signal to his neighbour.

"What's yer name, mite?"

"Geordie Kinloch."

"What's yer loin of business, Geordie?"

"Banking."

"Bastard."

"Excuse me?"

"Granted. Know why bankers have to be buried deeper in the earth than anyone else, Geordie?"

"Tell me."

"Cos deep down, they're quite nice." Cedric Sedgwick's guffaw filled the first-class cabin. Half a dozen investment bankers along the aisle cringed and burrowed deeper into their papers and laptops. This was going to be a long night. Geordie closed his book.

"So what's your business, Ced?"

"I'm South Pacific Regional Sales Co-ordinator for Matulinda." Cedric Sedgwick handed Geordie a laminated calling card with his photograph and address printed on it.

"Consumer electronics?"

"Partly. But it's our security electronic equipment that sells best in the Pacific. If the Tonga Defence Force buys it, Fiji's got to have it. If

Fiji gets it, the Solomons got to have it. If Nauru gets it, PNG has to get it. New Zealand has a huge contract with us. Counter-terrorism security electronics. Once they have it, then you sell them upgrades each year. It's like the Opium Wars. The natives get hooked on our gadgets." More guffaws.

"It sounds rather depressing."

"Naa. That's what makes the world go round. So what are you doing in Auckland?"

"I'm on the way to Los Angeles and thought I would take the scenic route."

"Been to New Zealand before?"

"Never."

"How long are you staying?"

"One day. I fly to Papeete tomorrow night after a day in Auckland."

"What're you planning to do for one day in New Zealand?"

"Oh, I'll look around Auckland, see some museums, shops and things."

"Auckland on Saturday's the most fat-arse boring city in the Southern hemisphere. Same Monday through Friday, mite. There's nothing to do there. Even a Pom would have trouble filling a day in Auckland." Cedric Sedgwick looked appalled by the idea of someone travelling 12,000 miles to spend one day in New Zealand, let alone Auckland.

"I'm sure I'll find something to do," Geordie replied. "There's the Sky Tower and the Bridge Walk. I can take a taxi to the North Shore Beaches. It's springtime. I'll go for a walk. There's the famous National Maritime Museum and a number of art galleries." He'd studied the brochures.

Cedric Sedgwick fell silent as Geordie returned pointedly to his book. Geordie was aware of his neighbour casting sideways glances, trying to figure him out. After dinner Ced reclined his seat and began snoring thunderously within minutes. Geordie wedged the airline's complimentary earplugs into his ears and dozed off as the silence filled his head.

The flight touched down in Auckland at first light. As they blearily gathered their belongings in the cabin, Cedric turned to Geordie, "Say, I've got our regional rep, Phil, meeting me off the plane. Want a lift down town?"

Unguardedly, Geordie replied, "That would be nice."

"He's a good man. He might have some idea what do in Auckland for a day."

If Cedric Sedgwick had Salesman tattooed on his forehead, Phil McQueen filled all available airspace like bagpipes in a nunnery. At the packed International Arrivals gate he hailed his boss from afar at the top of his voice, to everybody's irritation. Ced introduced his new companion. "Hey Phil. This is Geordie. He's a Pom. He's in New Zealand for one day. I offered him a ride downtown."

"One day in New Zealand? Yer kidding." Phil turned to Geordie, "I've got to take samples to some customers around town, then we go to Puhoi for lunch. That's up-country. You can come with us. You'll get to see a bit of New Zealand scenery."

"I have to be back at the airport by seven this evening for my flight to Papeete."

"No sweat, mite. I'll get you back here by five." To emphasize his point Phil pointed at the floor of the terminal. He led them to a maroon Chevy Camaro in the parking lot. He threw their bags in the trunk, Cedric sat in front, Geordie in the back, and they headed into Auckland. The day was like a summer day in Glasgow – grey clouds from horizon to horizon, cold, steady rain. "First, you get to see Auckland from a height, mite." He drove to a beauty spot overlooking the town. "The Maoris once had a fortress here. Best views in town."

They might have been surveying Clydeside in November. A party of

Japanese trippers disgorged from a bus into the rain, clicked their cameras dutifully and filed back aboard for the next beauty spot.

Most shops in downtown Auckland were either partly closed down with budget items on sale – cheap clothes, musical instruments and videos – or completely boarded up. The locals were poorly dressed, hard up and pinched. Most of the cars were old and driven maniacally by young turks wearing back-to-front baseball caps. Phil didn't seem to notice the fuming crates racing past him on blind summits and sharp corners, flashing their lights furiously at any vehicle ahead of them driving less than 20 mph above the speed limit.

Phil and Ced were engaged in sales talk for the entire journey. It gave Geordie a chance to inspect the sodden landscape as they sped by. They crossed The Bridge heading north, passing cheap housing and dreary settlements of blue-roofed bungalows. Phil detoured via pretty bays and beaches: "This is where we swim in the summer and set up the barbecue. While I mention it, Geordie, can you reach for the cooler on the seat beside you? Mine's a Jo Kuhtze. What about you, Ced? Geordie, help yourself."

It was nine in the morning as they snapped open the first beers of the day. It wasn't exactly what Geordie had in mind as homage to Ephraim Neuhoffer's memory. But maybe this was a more authentic New Zealand experience than shuffling reverently past Works of Art in an air-conditioned museum.

"Well folks, here we are." Phil belched loudly as he gunned, then cut, the Camaro's engine in a car park beside a large white wooden building. Its two Victorian storeys reminded Geordie of American colonial architecture. It had something of Connecticut about it; New Lyme, perhaps, or Mystic.

"Welcome to the Puhoi Pub."

They entered a large room containing an L-shaped bar and a high ceiling. It was tarred with a sticky brown glutinous décor that decades of tobacco smoke had bestowed on the room. About 30 people hung around in various groups, drinking pitchers of Red Lion Ale and pints of stout from bottles with yellow labels.

"Whaddyoo think, Geordie? We're completely in the boondocks here, 40 kilos from Auckland. The gentry don't venture out this far."

"Well, it's different. It's the real McCoy," Geordie had to agree, as he observed the hardware mounted on the walls. Shovels, spurs, spades, stirrups, saddles, boots, 8-foot pit saws, old logging photographs, miners' lamps, hurricane lamps, railway lamps, ship navigation lights, jars of Red Lion Ale, even a leather leg brace, were crammed on every available surface around the barroom walls.

The patron shuffled about the place in old slippers. He swayed and cussed and insulted his clientele, but because he was a character nobody seemed to mind. On the contrary, people loved him. Phil asked him for a light and the grizzled curmudgeon replied, "Gimme that cigarette." Phil gave him the fag, which was promptly scrunched up and thrown into the fire. "That'll light it for you, heh, heh, heh." Phil laughed nervously as the cantankerous old fart cackled and shuffled off to a distant corner of the bar.

Armed with jugs of beer, Ced Sedgwick and Phil ensconced themselves at the bar beside a group of tattooed Angels. The bikers were too far gone to be threatening. They sported leathers and long beards and dragged deeply on self-rolled smokes, but despite a generally menacing aura, they were actually just a group of paunchy old men. They exuded the faint sense of hostility characteristic of blue-collar bars everywhere in the world.

Geordie poured a Joseph Kuhtze Exhibition Lager and detached himself politely from Ced and Phil to explore the décor, much as a connoisseur might wander discreetly around a European drawing room with a whisky during a cocktail party. He examined the well-worn artefacts, the lumps of pine resin, tree stumps, ox heads, leather harnesses and clamps. A grey-muzzled, matted old sheepdog stood to welcome him before settling back down into the dust by the fire. Geordie began to see the poetry of the Puhoi Pub. At least the place had no affectations. It was genuinely filthy.

"Hey Geordie, come over here. Got some people wanna meet you." Phil came over and put an arm fraternally around his shoulder. Another Kuhtze lager was thrust into his hand. "Here, I want you to meet Angie and Jan."

"Delighted to meet you, Angie and Jan." The women were pear-shaped and short, in their late thirties. They had cropped hair, worn faces, bad teeth and rounded features. They wore black polyester slacks and white blouses which strained to accommodate their doughy chests.

"Where are you from, Geordie?"

"London and Scotland. What about you?"

"We're from Whangapanoa. How long are you in Puhoi for?"

"Just a few hours."

"Then where?"

"I'm going to Tahiti, then Los Angeles."

"How long you been in New Zealand?"

"About four hours."

"So you're only in New Zealand for one day?" Angie and Jan screeched in unison.

"Well, I suppose that's one way to look at it."

"Hey folks, this chep comes 12,000 miles from London to New Zealand for one day," they announced to everyone. Ced already had his arm around Jan.

Geordie was discomfited to suddenly become the centre of attraction in the crowded pub.

"We'd better give him something to remember us by."

Geordie smiled nervously and put up his hands in an appeasing gesture. "That won't be necessary. I'll never forget anything about Puhoi. It's an amazing place."

"How about a cuddle with the Assistant Manager of a dry-goods store in Whangapanaoa?" Angie patted his bottom. Geordie held her wrist firmly, to prevent further exploration of his nether regions. He glared at Phil, who grinned moronically, and said loudly, "You have to get me to the airport, Phil, I can't be late for my flight."

"Plenty of time yet, Geordie." Phil drained a full pint of Red Lion and shouted at the barman for another jug.

"Then give me your keys and I'll wait outside in the car."

"I'll wait with you, Geordie." Angie's teeth were black and rotted.

"No, that's OK, thanks." Alarmed, he detached himself firmly from Angie. "I'll wait outside on my own."

"OK, here's the keys, mite, we'll be outside in a few." Phil tossed a bunch of keys across the pub to Geordie.

It was raining hard as Geordie fumbled in the mud with the lock of the Camaro. He spread himself on the back seat, keeping a low profile in case Angie tried to find him in the car park, locking the car from inside as a precaution. He dozed off as the beers kicked in with his jet lag.

He was awakened by a tremendous commotion. A crowd of drunken revellers poured out of the Puhoi Pub. Entangled in a heaving scrum of limbs, heads, fists and ripping clothes Ced and Phil emerged and disappeared in the general melee like panicky swimmers in a rip tide. The scrummage tumbled towards the Camaro. Geordie unlocked the doors, leaped into the front seat, started the engine and pointed the car towards a rapid exit onto the highway. Phil broke away from the mob with Angie in hot pursuit. She was topless and flourished in his direction what seemed to be a broken bottle. She wore platform heels which did not offer much traction in the car park mud. Phil was 20 yards ahead of her. She floundered and screamed furiously in the morass. Phil reached the car, tore the passenger door open and threw himself on the front seat.

"In the name of mercy get the holy shit out of this place." Phil's clothes were ripped and filthy. A cut on his chin was bleeding heavily. "Geordie, drive straight into the mob, to hell with the car." He wound down his window. "I'll grab Ced and you drive like a fucking maniac away from this place. All right?"

"All right." Cedric's fists flailed like windmills into the faces and bellies of three pursuing tattooed bikers. Jan gripped him by one leg. He dragged her behind him, black with mud, alternately biting his calf and wailing like a banshee. Ced gave a mighty heave and she lost her grip, sprawling face downwards. He threw a stunning punch into the face of a bald Angel who fell squirming in the mud beside Jan. Ced half-dived and was half-pulled through the open car window. Phil grabbed him by the belt of his trousers and held him until he squirmed into the back seat.

As Geordie accelerated out of the car park Angie lunged at the windscreen. He had a vivid view of her muddied breasts slipping down the glass as she tried to find a grip. He shook her off the car by braking sharply. She flew off, landing on her backside in a pool of mud.

The Camaro fishtailed for a hundred yards along the road. When it was certain they were not being followed, Geordie slowed to the speed limit and slotted into the flow of traffic heading towards Auckland. A few minutes later two cop cars sped past them back towards Puhoi. Phil and Cedric were breathless from their escape, convulsing with laughter and reeking of beer.

"OK, gentlemen, what was that all about?"
"Jan was a biker's bird and Angie was Jan's bird."
"Lesbians? Why were they making a move on us, then?"
"Drunk bitches wanted a fight."
"I see. Glad I didn't take up Angie's offer to join me in the car park."

"Yeah. She'd a slit your throat and taken your money."

Phil and Cedric were in tatters. Their clothes were beyond repair, they were slathered in mud and both had multiple facial contusions. But they were too drunk to care and clearly found the whole thing quite hilarious. Geordie drove up to the International Departures Terminal at Auckland International Airport. As he removed his luggage from the trunk of the Camaro Ced mumbled incoherent goodbyes from the back seat. Phil got out and switched to the driver's seat. He handed Geordie a business card. "You played that well, mite. Next time you're in Auckland, remember to look us up. I know some good bars up-country."

"I'll bear that in mind. Thanks for being my tour guide today."

Phil grinned, patted Geordie's arm, and the muddy Camaro sped away from the terminal.

Two hours later Geordie was sitting in a spacious aisle seat in the first-class cabin of a New Zealand Airways jet. He'd taken a shower in the Executive Lounge and felt clean, tired and pleasantly mellow, satisfied that he'd done credit to Ephraim Neuhoffer's memory. As the flight attendant topped up his glass with champagne his neighbour annoyed him with small talk.

"So, were you in New Zealand on business?"

"Yes, as a matter of fact."

"What's your line of business?"

"Investment banking."

"Good opportunities in New Zealand?"

"They're tough negotiators, but sometimes you just have to walk away."

"I've heard that the world's top bankers come over here expecting to find a country full of hillbillies" the New Zealander replied proudly, "and they're amazed when they find they're dealing with some very sophisticated minds."

Geordie raised the glass to his neighbour. "So I discovered."

Chapter 2

Chicago Burns

It was as cold as it gets that January night. A line of limousines drew up on the hotel ramp, delivering folks from City Hall and the wire houses and commodity traders of South LaSalle Street. Thick swirls of exhaust fumes crystallized in the deadly wind-chill. The women wore deep fur coats over long elegant dresses, clutching silver and gold cocktail bags. In the arctic blast one brave gal showed a flash of leg for the photographers as she slid out of her limo and sashayed across the frozen sidewalk into the warm lobby.

The men were something else. All of them – from fat bald aldermen to senior black cops, from corporate chief executives to locally acclaimed celebrities – all of them wore kilts and Highland jackets. They were uneasy. It doesn't come natural to calloused Chicago politicians and businessmen to wear skirts in January.

They separated into two crowds: the women in a chattering miasma of hair lacquer and sweet perfume at the foot of the ballroom steps; the men in line waiting gingerly to hand fur coats over to the check lady. They reassembled and made their way up the staircase to the reception. Busty girls in short kilts and plastic smiles waited on the top step, holding silver trays of double-measure single malts.

"Highland or Island, Sir?"

"Whazza difference?"

"Highland's light and smooth as a summer glen, Island's dark and smoky like a winter fire."

"Gimme a shot of Highland" said the black alderman to enthusiastic jibes from his retinue. He grabbed a glass and threw the silky liquid back into his tonsils. He smacked his lips, held the glass up to the light and rolled his eyes in mockery of a wine aficionado.

"Now gimme a shot of the Island." He picked out a glass of the darker whisky and downed it in one. He repeated his connoisseur act. "Yep," he decided, "I'll stick to the Island." He lifted his third shot glass from the tray and joined the crowd milling about at the top of the staircase.

Four hundred guests gathered on the floor outside the ballroom. The centrepiece of the heavily gilded mezzanine floor was a cherubimed faux Louis XV table surmounted by a man-sized Chinese vase. It was filled with a cascade of blue and white flowers in honour of St Andrew, patron saint of Scotland.

A multi-tiered chandelier hung directly above the eight-foot flower arrangement. It ensured that Scotland's translucent colours were the undisputed focus of the room, for those who were conscious enough of the occasion to figure it out.

The volume rose steadily and blue cigar smoke curled high above the guffawing whisky-fuelled mob of Chicago Scots-for-a-night. At the strike of seven, the skirl of a bagpipe silenced the crowd. The doors of the ballroom swung open, and 10 kilted pipers flanked the entrance, playing *Scotland the Brave*.

The Master of Ceremonies was a bearded Highlander. He shouted at the crowd like a drill sergeant.

"Guid evening, ladies and gentlemen. Would everryone please take their place for dinner in the Ballrume. If ye havnae seen it a'ready the table seatin' plan is to the left o' the staircase."

Geordie Kinloch was the guest of a veteran Chicago politician who was thrilled, for his own agenda, to have a real-life Scot at the high table. Geordie wore his full dress kilt, sporting a venerable moth-eaten sporran that, among other excitements, had seen action at Magersfontein with the Gordon Highlanders a hundred years earlier. He picked his way through rows of tables festooned with blue and white flower decorations.

Ladies' places were marked by a small St Andrews flag, men's by a Scottish Lion Rampant. Man-sized bottles of Cardhu, Lochnagar, Macallan and Laphroaig malt were placed in the centre of each table, a bottle of Strathmore water was at each place. Candles were lit, silver and glassware sparkled, pipers played. The ballroom was spectacularly decked out for the Sixteenth Annual Chicago Robert Burns Supper.

To Geordie's left sat an eminent sculptor, most famous for a panoramic suite of figures on the terrace of Chicago's exclusive West Bank Club. To his right was Len McQuarie, Chairman of the Burns Committee and organizer of the event. Len stood up and took the microphone when everyone was in position.

"I would like to accord the warmest welcome to our distinguished friends and guests who have come all this way to attend the Sixteenth Annual Chicago Robert Burns Supper. Many of you have travelled from distant parts of the United States and Canada for this event . . . "

"Yea, and Springfield, Illinois!" a drunk interjected to localized applause.

Len McQuarie coughed politely, ". . . but I would like to reserve my most cordial welcome for our guests who have travelled all the way from Scotland to attend this event tonight."

A drunken cheer rose from the left of the ballroom.

"Thank you. Now I'd appreciate if everyone would bow their heads as the Reverend Easton McLean says grace to open the proceedings." He handed the microphone to the Reverend McLean, a ruddy-faced minister of the Kirk. He began.

"Some hae meat and canna eat
and some wad eat that want it . . ."

"Speak in English, mun," a slurred voice yelled from the back, followed by loud hushes and giggles from across the room. The minister's voice rose above the commotion.

"But we hae meat and we can eat
And sae the Lord be thankit."

Reverend McLean bowed and sat down. It was the signal for scores of waiters and waitresses to march out of the kitchen and fan out between the tables serving Rabbit Terrine and Smoked Salmon. The volume settled down as hundreds of hungry people attacked the food on their plates. The first course was followed seamlessly by Pheasant Consommé and Quenelles.

"The guys at this hotel know how to handle a crowd," Len remarked to the people around him at the table. "When things get raucous, you just gotta feed 'em."

"I thought things were about to get out of hand for a moment," Geordie observed.

"Yea, the pols in this room should pay attention. Only hungry people revolt," Eminent Sculptor chimed in.

"So Geordie, how long are you in America for?"

"I'm here mainly for this event. I'm going on to Kansas City afterwards, then back to Scotland at the end of the week."

"That's a lot of travel in a short time."

Before Geordie could keep filling the empty bucket of small-talk, a deep groan rose from the bowels of the hotel. The ballroom went mute as the excruciating noise of revving bagpipes evolved into a stirring Highland tune. Pipe Sergeant Jim McInlay appeared out of the kitchen in his full kilted glory, marching slowly in front of two liveried chefs bearing a silver platter upon which sat a thing resembling an oversized condom filled with porridge.

The piper led the procession around the ballroom to allow everyone to admire their imminent meal. Geordie wondered how enough haggis to feed 400 guests had been procured in Chicago without breaking every conceivable federal, city and state food safety directive.

By now many bottles of Cardhu and Lochnagar had been drained. The level of noise and male raucousness was rising to a pitch. Len McQuarie tapped his glass by the microphone. The roar diminished.

"And now . . . "

"Hey McQuarie, you asshole."

"And now," he ignored the heckler, "I give you The Ode To a Haggis by Robert Burns." Desultory claps, catcalls and cheers. Len McQuarie began:

"Fair fa' your honest, sonsie face,
Great chieftain o' the pudding-race!
Aboon them a' ye take your place,"

"You take your place, McQuarie!" The man shouted with a laugh. Many had obviously drunk heavily before the event began. The bastards had even heckled dear old Reverend McLean through the Selkirk Grace. They treated the whole thing as a joke, but in that deadly, drunken humourlessness that often leads to trouble.

McQuarie skipped a few lines, waved a knife in the direction of his heckler and intoned:

"His knife see rustic labour dight
An' cut you up with ready slight,
Trenching your gushing entrails bright
Like onie ditch
And then, O what a glorious sight,
Warm-reekin, rich!"

With a savage grin he plunged the knife into the guts of the haggis. There was little doubt who he was thinking about as he stabbed it violently again and again. The chefs carried the mutilated delicacy back to the kitchen. Minutes later it returned on plates and the steaming mess was served, accompanied with mashed potatoes and turnips, to the crowd.

A guest from the high table stood to propose a toast. He was drowned in the uproar from the back tables. It was then the turn of a distinguished speaker to talk about 'The Land They Came To'. His name was James McIntyre, a revered columnist from a Chicago newspaper. He was a tall, athletic man in late middle age, with a beard and kindly blue eyes. He began,

"The Mary Rose left Loch Arkaig in May 1778, bound for Nova Scotia. Its passengers included 11 families from one village in the West Highlands who decided there was no further future for them in Scotland."

A fat bald man yelled "Losers!"

James MacIntyre ignored the comment. He continued: "The head of one family was called David MacIntyre. He was a man of 30 with a pregnant wife, a small son and two daughters. David was my great, great, great, great grandfather."

"Big deal, mun! Get on with the story."

"When the Mary Rose arrived in Nova Scotia there was a cholera epidemic in Halifax. The families were only permitted to disembark in a cove 30 miles down the coast. There were no roads, no houses, no food . . ."

MacIntyre continued in this vein, describing his ancestors' adventures across Canada to a mining camp in Montana, fighting in the American Civil War, the First World War, the Great Depression, the Second World War and Vietnam. It was a thrilling family history. But for the loutish heckling, it would have been worthy of a Public Radio broadcast. After delivering his 10-minute talk, MacIntyre retired to his seat at the top table, looking hurt. Geordie felt for the man: he was clearly a sensitive soul who had just been cut to ribbons.

The keynote speech was 'The Immortal Memory', to be delivered by Alderman Rakowski. A Scot for the day, he tapped the microphone until he commanded everyone's attention. There was a momentary silence, during which he announced 'It's a pity Robert Burns wasn't Italian,' which caused a further uproar. Alderman Rakowski walked across to Len McQuarie, shook his hand, returned to the microphone and said, "I'm not gonna waste my time speaking to this bunch of drunk Scotch assholes. I'm outta here." He walked straight through the length of the ballroom and out of the door. For the first time that evening silence fell on the proceedings. Len was aghast.

"Rakowski was our keynote speaker. He's shafted us." Len leaned down the table imploring desperately, "Can anyone here speak on a Scottish subject for twenny minutes?" People looked at their finger nails and fiddled with cutlery on the table, avoiding eye contact at all costs. "Geordie? Geordie – you're the most true Scot at the high table. You live there. Can you talk about a Scottish subject for twenny minutes?"

Geordie's heart took a flip when he realized he couldn't back out of this one. He played cool, "Sure, what do you want me to talk about?"

"Something of Scotch interest, preferably to do with Robert Burns."

"I could tell some shaggy-dog stories about Scotland. They're not original, but they may work."

"Sure, sure, Geordie. Anything Scottish. You're on."

Geordie Kinloch would have felt more relaxed if he had been caught naked in the shower with a vicar's wife. His legs weakened, but he strode confidently up to the podium. The din was deafening. He grabbed the microphone and shouted at the top of his voice, "Shut the Fuck up!"

To his amazement, 400 rowdy souls fell silent.

"You should be ashamed of yourselves. A lot of people have made a big effort to make this a lovely evening. You yelled down one of the toast proposers, you interrupted the Reverend Easton McLean, you abused James MacIntyre and now you've yelled down Alderman Rakowski. I strongly suggest that if anyone here would prefer to be somewhere else, you should leave the room now."

Geordie stood silently for 15 seconds. It felt like an hour. "Nobody? Right. Do me the favour of behaving yourselves and let's make the rest of this evening a pleasant experience for everyone."

Len McQuarie grinned. He and James MacIntyre led a round of applause.

"I don't have a prepared speech but I'm going to tell you three Scottish anecdotes. Some might call them jokes, and I apologize if you've heard them before." Geordie's head was racing to find a story he could tell that was in the spirit of the evening. Something that was amusing but not too smutty. Despite the volume of whisky consumed there were sure to be folks out there with tender sensibilities. He remembered a story he'd heard in his car on a BBC Radio Burns Night Special, five years earlier.

"My first anecdote is about a recent trip by a member of the British Royal Family to open the new wing of a hospital. After cutting the ribbon Her Royal Highness was escorted around the new state-of-the-art facility by the Chief Registrar of the hospital. In a special ward, she stopped at a bed and asked the patient how he was. He replied:

"Now bank an' brae are claith'd in green
An' scatter'd cowslips sweetly spring . . ."

Her Royal Highness looked nonplussed. They strolled past a few more beds and she stopped beside another patient: "And how are you enjoying these wonderful new facilities?"

"Gie me the lonely valley,
The dewy eve, and rising moon . . . "

Her Royal Highness looked puzzled, but smiled serenely. The party moved on through the ward, stopping at one last bed. Before Her Royal Highness could ask the question, the man in the bed spouted:

"Wee, sleekit, cow'rin, timorous beastie
O what a panic's in thy breastie!"

Her Royal Highness, by this stage, was thoroughly confused. She turned to the Chief Registrar and asked, "What was that all about?"

"Oh, your Royal Highness, I should have explained. We've just been on a tour of the Serious Burns Unit of the hospital.'"

Geordie had loved this joke from the moment he'd heard it, tucking it away to tell in the future in sophisticated company. Just like tonight.

But apart from scattered laughs, a few polite coughs and the general murmur of cutlery on crockery, the crowd was silent. Geordie looked across at Len who had a bilious expression on his face.

"Serious Burns Unit, folks, Serious Burns." Geordie tried desperately to salvage the joke. He paused. "Well, I have another Scottish anecdote that you might appreciate."

Len nodded encouragingly.

"Auld Jock was 90 and lay dying in his cottage in the glens near Auchtermuchty. He got his son to summon his oldest friend, Mac, from the glen over the hill. The octogenarian duly made his way to Jock's cottage and sat by his friend's bedside.

"Oh Mac, my dear friend. Will you do me the greatest favour when I die?"

"Och, aye, Jock. I'll do innything you ask."

"Even somethin' I couldna trust ma own son to do?"

"Och, aye, Jock. I'll do innything you ask."

"See that cupboard over there?"

"Aye, Jock, I see it."

"If you go to that cupboard and open it, you will find a bottle of hindred-year-old single malt that I wus keepin' for ma hindredth birthday."

Mac shuffled over to the cupboard. He searched carefully through a pile of clothes and duly found a green bottle with a wax-sealed top. It had a handwritten label by Dan Mackinnon, Chief Distiller, certifying that the whisky was distilled on March 11th 1860, matured in an oak cask, then bottled and sealed 'on the premises' on March 12th 1960.

"Is this the whusky, Jock?" Mac asked.

"Aye, that's the whisky."

"Jock, I canna tell you how much this means tae me. That you would hold this whusky back and give it tae your best friend on yer deithbed." A tear came to Mac's rheumy eye.

"Nae sae fast, Mac. You promised you wud do innything I asked."

"Innything at all, Jock."

"When I die, I want you to open that bottle and pour it over my grave."

"Oh Jock, my dear auld Jock. Of course I'll do that thing for ye. But I have one favour to ask of you now, Jock."

"Innything at all, Mac, innything at all."

"Do ye mind if I pass it through ma kidneys first?'"

This joke had more support than the first, particularly among the more raucous elements who had guzzled their way through four bottles of whisky on their tables. Geordie was redeemed. Len beamed.

"I would be happy to share more Scottish jokes with you over a few whiskies after dinner, but in the meantime I'm going to hand the proceedings back to Len McQuarie. Thank you."

Geordie passed the microphone back to Len and took his seat back at the high table. Len thanked Geordie, bade everyone to enjoy the next course and sat down. Waiters and waitresses again fanned out through the tables, dispensing Roastit Stirk and Leek Pie.

Shouting and abuse continued from the same troublesome corner. James MacIntyre bowed gently to his neighbours and pushed back his chair, "Excuse me. I'll be right back." He negotiated purposefully down the crowded aisles, stopping to talk to friends at several tables on the way.

He reached the furthest table and calmly tapped the fat bald man on the shoulder. As the unsuspecting fellow turned round, James MacIntyre delivered a jackhammer punch into his face. Straight out of an old time Western, the fat bald man reeled backwards in his chair, ass over apex, and fell with a resounding crash on his back. Blood poured from his nose and a cut upper lip.

Surprise was complete. MacIntyre bowed to the man's astonished dining companions, smiled and started to make his way back to the high table. Cheers and catcalls rose in equal numbers from the crowd.

For a man who weighed well north of 250 pounds, the victim picked himself off the floor with astonishing alacrity and launched himself with a demented roar across the ballroom. He floored James MacIntyre like a bag of cement, crashing into two tables on the way. Bottles, cutlery, vases of flowers, handbags, chairs, half-eaten plates of Roastit Stirk and whisky glasses exploded across the floor. Women screamed, fists flailed, kilts ripped, sporrans flew, collars tore, blood ran.

Men from all sides leaped up to separate them. MacIntyre detached himself from the melee – studs ripped out of his shirt, the left arm of his jacket hanging by a thread, his silver hair tousled – and walked unsteadily out of the room. The fat bald fellow was spitting blood. He broke away from his restraining pals and staggered across the ballroom in pursuit of MacIntyre. He reminded Geordie of a wounded gorilla, only drunk and less intelligent.

The crowd followed and spilled out of the ballroom into the mezzanine where the scrap erupted into a full-scale brawl. City politicians whacked each other every which way, black on black,

black on white, white on black, white on white, fuelled by high-octane whisky. After one spectacular punch, an off-duty senior cop reeled backwards into the Louis XV table and smashed its gilded leg. The Chinese vase teetered, tilted fatally with the collapsing table and shattered with an almighty crash as it hit the parquet floor. Gallons of water and soaking flowers were scattered over a wide area, rapidly turning into blue and white puree as bodies skidded in all directions.

Geordie was an onlooker. He was not drunk, nor was he partisan except for a passing sympathy for MacIntyre. He stood on the edge of the mezzanine floor with his back to the wall. Shameful to admit, he cheered as the great and good citizens of the Windy City laid into each other. He shouted to the Eminent Sculptor, who was also enjoying the spectacle from the safety of the back wall, "They are simply NOT going to believe this when I tell them back home!"

Eminent Sculptor replied, "Rabbie Burns would have loved this crazy, brawling, whisky-fuelled mayhem. Chicago meets Scotland meets malt whisky meets Burns. Don'tcha love it?"

Len McQuarie was hysterical. His prize, his baby, the Sixteenth Annual Chicago Robert Burns Supper, had degenerated into an almighty riot which threatened to drag every skeleton out of Chicago's overstuffed closet. Cops were hitting churchmen; politicians were thrashing each other, stockbrokers clobbered lawyers. Women tore at their menfolk to stop fighting. They were elbowed aside then jumped right back into the fray, evening gowns in tatters. Len ran back into the kitchens, returning with a platoon of chefs and busboys wielding frying pans.

The fire alarm went off. Within seconds, high pressure spray filled the mezzanine, instantly soaking everybody and everything. Geordie's wretched sporran was drenched, adding a chapter to its illustrious history. The cops and the fire brigade arrived. The spray was turned off. A groaning mush of humanity picked itself off the floor. The cops and firemen immediately saw that many senior-ranking cops and firemen were at the party. Instead of wading in with truncheons and handcuffs they politely helped their groaning colleagues to their feet and put away their notebooks and cameras.

Geordie bade goodnight to his hysterical host and collected his coat. His clothes froze instantly in the wind-chill but he managed to flag a taxi quickly on Michigan Avenue, heading South to his hotel.

He was awakened at eight. A trolley was wheeled into his room bearing coffee, warm blueberry muffins, croissants and a Denver omelette. The attendant drew back the curtains to reveal a brilliant blue day from the 25th floor of his hotel, overlooking the Chicago River and the skyscrapers beyond. Crowds streamed across Michigan Avenue Bridge on their way to work towards Wacker and the Loop.

A morning newspaper lay on Geordie's breakfast trolley. He flicked through to read about the night's riotous events. He eventually found a column in the Social Page entitled 'Chicago honors Scottish Bard'. The article described the elegance of the evening, the formalities of Piping the Haggis and the good-natured toasts and poems read out during the meal. It gave a brief Who's Who of attendees, including multiple politicians and industrial titans from the city, concluding, 'The resounding success of the Sixteenth Annual Chicago Robert Burns Supper was testament to the excellent communication that exists between all the strands of city life. Robert Burns would be proud that such an event was held in his name.' The article was written by one James MacIntyre.

Chapter 3

The Shard of Pottery

The Land Cruiser nosed carefully out of the leafy hotel compound into the chaos, stench and choking red dust of the marketplace. Here, men were heaving sacks of sorghum off overloaded donkey carts and women were raising colourful awnings for their stalls. They were setting out piles of sesame cakes, plastic teapots, flip-flops, chilli peppers, *piment africain* and a colourful array of unrecognizable fruits and vegetables, all in the hope of selling enough to feed their families that day.

It was seven in the morning. Already the coolness of the night was being devoured by the equatorial heat. It had rained overnight, but that merely kept down the dust until the dampness steamed off at sunrise.

They drove slowly through the market and edged down a rutted track to the south of Banfora. A steady inflow of people headed towards them on both sides of the track. Boys pulled carts piled high with firewood, women walked in procession, elegantly balancing on their heads enamel bowls brimming with papayas, tomatoes, dried fish, gourds and kitchenware. Most of the women had infants strapped to their backs. Men rode into town on bicycles or wove precariously on their mopeds, spewing a foul cocktail of exhaust gases into the town's lungs.

The road crossed the rickety railway track which ran from Bobo Dioulasso to Abidjan and opened into a wide red highway flanked on each side by enormous broadleaved trees spreading their shade for travellers.

"*L'héritage coloniale.*" Kaya jerked his thumb towards a massive baobab tree.

"*Oui?*" Geordie recalled the millions of poplars and plane trees stretching along the roads of France. This was the tropical equivalent. From the passenger seat he studied Kaya, his driver, guide and companion for the past 10 days. He was a handsome man in his 40s, lean and muscular with strong facial features. Three Mossi tribal scars ran parallel on each side of his face from his cheekbones to his mouth. He wore a Dodgers tee shirt, a gift from one of the well-meaning aid sources who roamed around his country Doing Good. He was educated, fluent in French and keen to practise his English on Geordie whenever he could.

The foliage began to thicken in the landscape. It was greener and denser than in the north around Ouagadougou. Fast-flowing water surged through culverts, eager to race downstream towards Ghana and the Volta Basin. Villages were becoming less visible from the road, screened by the luxuriant undergrowth.

Geordie had been on an intense schedule since arriving in Burkina Faso 10 days earlier. The bank had sent him to undertake two feasibility studies: one for a manganese mine north in the Sahel and the other for an irrigation project in the southwest. He accepted the assignment with alacrity. How often does a fellow get to visit such an exotic country on business?

An immediate problem he'd faced on arrival was the distance between the projects whose feasibility he was there to study. The manganese mine in the Sahel was 500km north of the capital on the border with Mali. The irrigation project was 1000km in the opposite direction, along frightful roads, on the border with Côte d'Ivoire. It was as if he'd been ordered to drive from London to Edinburgh, then back to Penzance, on cart tracks, all in a week. He'd made enquiries and was discouraged from flying – 'Aircraft are known to disappear in the bush, monsieur' – so he'd hired Kaya and his Land Cruiser for the duration of his visit.

The roads were mainly of hard corrugated red earth, but in an attempt to curry favour with Burkina Faso's dictator the Taiwanese government and the European Union had paid to put down tarmac for a few kilometres here and there. The tarmac was always welcome but made the bone-rattling experience of the rutted track even worse when it resumed.

Today, Geordie was free until the evening. He was due to meet three business contacts for an early dinner. He wanted to use the gift of a spare day to relax and explore the country. After studying a guidebook to Burkina Faso he asked Kaya to drive him to an area known as the Pics de Sandou.

Kaya pleaded that the area was too far and difficult to reach. "Besides, there are bandits all round the Pics de Sandou and refugees from the civil war in Côte d'Ivoire." Anticipating that he had trumped Geordie's plans, Kaya sat back in the car seat and waited for a more sensible suggestion.

"No Kaya, we're going to the Pics de Sandou. They look like an interesting place to visit. We'll tell the hotel where we're going and if we're not back by six this evening they can alert the police."

"*Ou l'armée.*" Kaya responded glumly.

Geordie's spirits rose as the countryside became prettier with each passing mile. Kaya looked sullen, clenching his jaws as they tooled along. He was normally chatty, but this morning he wasn't happy.

"Look! Kaya, can you stop? I want to take a photograph." They'd just passed a sign for a village called Voulu Zonga. Set back from the road, it looked like a Smurf settlement. Round huts of various sizes with conical thatched roofs were clustered together, completely enclosed by a mud wall. Goats grazed by the entrance gate.

"Quintessential Africa, isn't it?"

Kaya was expressionless. Continuing to face forwards he slowed the car to walking pace. "Tell me when you have the right position for your photograph."

"Here's fine." Kaya stopped. Without leaving the vehicle Geordie leaned out of the window, lined up his camera, carefully adjusted the telephoto lens and pushed the button. It wouldn't click. He tried again. It failed to click again.

"*Merde*! Never mind, Kaya, drive on. I must have forgotten to do something with the camera. I'll check it and get a photo when we return later." Kaya looked relieved as he speeded up and left Voulu Zonga behind them. Geordie checked the buttons and dials of the digital camera.

"M/A – no. M – yes. VR – off. Format – standard." Geordie pointed the camera at the moving roadside and clicked. "That's odd, it works perfectly well now. I don't know what the problem was."

"Monsieur Kinloch, we will be at the Pics de Sandou in 15 minutes. You must listen to me carefully."

Geordie looked up, startled to hear Kaya address him in such portentous tones. "What is it, Kaya?"

"The Pics de Sandou are the sacred ground of the Senoufo *animistes*. Just like Mussulmans have their holy mosques and Chrétiens have their holy churches, so the Senoufo *animistes* have the Pics de Sandou."

"What's the story of the Senoufo animists?"

"The Senoufo are a tribe of farmers. They live only in this small part of Burkina Faso and across the border in Côte d'Ivoire and Mali. Honour goes to the best farmer in each village. The man who grows best becomes a tribal elder. They understand plants and they're *animistes*."

"What are *animists*?"

"*Animisme* is the dominant religion in Africa, followed by Islam and Chrétiens. *Moi, je suis catholique.* My parents were *animistes*. We all believe there is one God. The Mussulman approaches God through the prophet Mohammed. The Chrétien approaches God through the prophet Jesus Christ. The *animiste* approaches God through objects."

"What kind of objects?"

"Any objects that connect you to your ancestor spirits. You must perform rituals around the object. If you perform a ritual wrong the spirit gets very angry. Then you get a big problem, like no babies, drought and sickness."

"I still don't understand what sort of object."

"The object can be natural, like a *caillou* . . . what do you say?"

"A pebble."

"Yes, a pebble. Or a piece of wood. Or it can be made by man, like a doll, a mask or a spoon. A *sorcier* or a *féticheur* gives it the power of the spirit and you worship it to stay close to your ancestors."

"So you might worship a spoon?" Geordie tried not to sound too incredulous.

"Yes, but the spoon is your road to God, not God himself."

"And there is a lot of ritual around the spoon?"

"*Oui, certainement.* The danger is that any object, anywhere, any time may have the *grigri*, so you must respect all things at all times."

"The *grigri*?"

"Filled with the spirit of ancestors."

"Christians would regard this as a load of superstition," Geordie commented, feeling from the way Kaya talked that this was a most unsatisfactory religion.

Kaya smiled. "Half an hour ago you tried to take a photograph at Voulu Zonga."

"So?"

"So the *sorcier*'s spell stops strangers from interfering with the spirit of the village."

"What nonsense!"

"It is real, monsieur. If we go back the same way we will stop and ask the *sorcier* to lift the spell. You will then be able to take your photograph."

Geordie fell silent. The road was becoming hilly and twisty. They reached a beaten-up, peeling sign partly obscured by the undergrowth. He could make out the words, *Vous Souhaite la Bienvenue aux Pics de Sandou.*

A few hundred yards beyond the sign they came to a flat-roofed hut by the roadside. A mat of grass thatch lay on the roof to absorb the relentless heat of the sun. A table was the only piece of furniture in the hut. A man lay asleep on it. Kaya stopped the Land Cruiser and walked over to him. He sat up with a start. Geordie was just behind Kaya.

"*Que voulez-vous?*" the man asked.

"*Mon ami,*" Kaya began, "My friend here wants a tour of the Pics de Sandou." He turned round and pointed back at Geordie with his thumb.

"I am the official guide of the Pics de Sandou." The man jumped off the table. "My name is Moka. The tour costs a thousand francs."

"How long is the tour?" Geordie asked the man, who was short and powerfully built. The ethnic differences between the Senoufo and Mossi tribesmen were marked. His features were rounder than Kaya's; his skin was so black it was almost blue. He was compact, with the build of a weightlifter, compared to Kaya who was tall and slender like a marathon runner.

"One hour, three kilometres. I take you on a circle." Moka pointed at the range of hills that disappeared into the distance. They would cover only a fraction of the hills.

Kaya arched his eyebrow at Geordie, "Well?"

"Sounds fine to me. Are you coming?"

"No. I wait here."

Geordie donned a broad-brimmed conical hat that he'd bought in the Sahel from a Taureg tribesman, took a litre bottle of Lafi mineral water from the cooler and slung the camera around his neck. "Right. Let's go."

"Monsieur, before we go, you must listen carefully," Moka began. "Les Pics de Sandou are a sacred place to the Senoufo animists. You must walk where I walk, do not go away from me, do not touch any plants and do not pick anything up from the ground."

This was the second time in half an hour that Geordie had been lectured about the sanctity of animism. "Of course, I'll follow your instructions."

"*Très bien*, come with me." Moka struck out along a path through deep dry grass. Before vanishing into the bush, Geordie looked back at Kaya; he was leaning against the front of the Land Cruiser. He waved and shouted back at him, "In one hour!"

The path rose steeply through a gorge of blackened sandstone eroded into grotesque shapes. It opened into a natural amphitheatre. Moka explained that young Senoufo men began their initiation here. When they reach the age of 14, they are brought to these hills for 10 days without food or water. They are taught tribal dances and religious incantations, shown how to find food, hunt and locate water.

"Every plant in the Pics de Sandou is important." Moka picked a tiny star-shaped white flower from a bush in a crevice in the rocks. "This one, you crush it in your fingers and rub it in your eyes. It takes out the dirt from your eyes." Moka did as he said, rubbing the pulp from the flower into his eyes. Geordie didn't imitate him, but Moka smiled, "Ah, *c'est bien*. That feels good."

"What about this one?" Geordie reached out to finger the succulent leaves of a tall, gangly cactus.

"NON!" Moka pulled Geordie away from the plant. "This we use to protect our village from enemies. We dip arrows in the juice of the plant. One scratch, you die." The cacti were spread out in a wide arc on both sides of the path. If Moka were telling the truth, Geordie would be doomed if he wandered off the trail.

They reached a plateau where the overgrown foundations of a

deserted village could be seen. "Round huts were for women. They symbolize fertility. The square huts were for men. The round huts had a big pot built into the wall over here . . ." Moka pointed to a recess on the left of a doorway. ". . . and a fetish built into the wall on the right, to protect the people in the house."

They walked a wide loop through the sandstone canyons of the Pics de Sandou. The temperature was crushing, about 40 degrees. Geordie finished his water. At times he fancied that some pinnacles and rock features had been sculpted by humans. Some looked like faces, some were wonderfully phallic, some cracks in the rocks were highly suggestive of the female anatomy.

"Moka, when young men come here for their initiation rites, do you give them plants which make them high?"

"*Mais oui.*" Moka reached into the branches of a tree and picked a fruit that looked like a pear. "Eat this and you will see the spirits of your ancestors."

"We use whisky for the same purpose."

"*Ah oui?*"

Moka led Geordie to a rocky outcrop that overlooked a dense forest to the west. The cliff was at least 300 feet high. "This is a sacred place for sacrifice. Côte d'Ivoire is over there."

"What kind of sacrifice?"

"Sheep, goats, cows, people sometimes."

"People?"

"Oui. Our enemies, to please god."

The place had a baleful atmosphere. Geordie imagined their terror as sacrificial victims were flung off the edge onto the rocks far below. "How long ago?"

Expecting Moka to be referring to ancient times, Geordie was surprised at the response:

"Last year, the Senoufo sacrificed enemies from Côte d'Ivoire here."

"How many?" Geordie affected nonchalance.

"Twenty, maybe thirty."

"Good lord. Isn't that illegal?"

"So is rape, stealing and murder. They were punished for their crimes and sacrificed to please God."

Geordie tried to imagine what it must have felt like being dragged along this path and hurled over the cliffs.

As they turned to head back towards their starting point, Geordie spotted a small triangular shard of pottery in the grass by the path. He picked it up. It was of reddish clay with white embedded speckles. It looked like part of the rim of an ancient pot with a slight lip on the outside. A crude herringbone pattern was etched into the clay, but it was otherwise no more remarkable than a chip off a flowerpot. He slipped it into his pocket.

Geordie was relieved to see Kaya waiting in the Land Cruiser. The windows were closed and the air conditioning operated at full blast He paid Moka, thanked him for a most interesting tour, shook hands and clambered into the cool relief of the car.

They returned along the red dusty road. The sun was at its highest and Geordie was extremely grateful to the foresighted French colonial administrators for planting their trees a century earlier. The road was like a cool tunnel passing through the steamy landscape. When they reached Voulu Zonga, Kaya stopped the car on the verge. He said, "Stay here, I return in a few minutes."

Kaya sauntered along the track and disappeared through the gates of the village. Twenty minutes later he re-emerged with a grin on his face. He announced, "It is OK for you now to take a photograph of Voulu Zonga. I gave the sorcier 1000 francs and he lifted the spell." It was Geordie's turn to arch an eyebrow at Kaya. He lined up his camera and clicked. He checked the digital display panel: it showed a perfect photograph of the Smurf village.

The road from Banfora to Bobo Dioulasso was surfaced with tarmac, courtesy, for some reason, of the European taxpayer, *'pour votre confort'*. Geordie dozed as they barrelled along and wasn't really aware of the journey. They reached the hotel at five o'clock. L'Auberge was the most civilized hotel he had encountered in Burkina Faso. Immediately after checking into his room Geordie went swimming in the magnificent pool. He was alone but for a woolly black dog pacing up and down beside him along the edge as he swam his laps. An African Grey parrot sat on the bar, screeching obscenities in French to the world at large. The hotel was wonderfully French colonial, like a backdrop from Beau Geste or Casablanca.

Hors d'oeuvres were set out under an awning on the patio. Geordie's guests were two African engineers from a local irrigation project and an Italian agronomist attached to a FAO mission to the Province of Comoe. The purpose of the dinner was to understand the potential for financing agricultural projects in the region. Geordie had seen family rice paddies and a few industrial-scale sugar cane fields with irrigation booms, but needed to understand the scope for further investing in the area.

Two chilled bottles of Lafi mineral water and four litre bottles of SO.B. BRA beer were placed on the table. "*À votre santé.*" Geordie lifted his glass to his guests. He turned to one of the African engineers to ask his perspective on a project. He looked intensely at the man's face but couldn't focus on his features. It was as if he were looking at a shapeless cloud. The man's face had gone.

He turned to his colleague. It was the same. He looked over to the Italian. All he could discern was a disembodied smile. It was like staring at a surrealist painting. He couldn't make out what was being said. He looked down at his hand holding the glass of beer. It was distant, like looking through the wrong end of a telescope. It didn't belong to him. He tried to get up. "Will . . . you . . . excuse me please?"

Geordie woke to the rhythmic churning of a fan in the ceiling above the bed. A dim light shone through the slatted windows from the courtyard. He lay soaking in sweat, flat and immobile; his head pounded. He had been stripped of his clothes and wrapped in a white sheet, like a shroud. He must have moaned when he woke up, because Kaya entered the room.

"*Ça va*, Geordie?"

Geordie simply looked at him. He was too weak to talk.

"I don't know if you have malaria – or something else." Kaya flipped a small object in the air. "This fell out of your pocket. What is it?"

Geordie couldn't talk. His eyes widened as he recognized the shard of pottery he'd picked up that morning.

"What is this, Geordie? I need to know. It has strong *grigri*. *Très, très fort*."

Geordie turned his head away but the suddenness of the gesture told Kaya what he needed to know. "Did Moka, your guide at the Pics de Sandou, tell you not to touch anything?"

Geordie managed a faint nod.

"Did Moka tell you he was a *féticheur*?"

Geordie shook his head. Kaya looked frightened.

"A *féticheur* talks to the spirits through objects. Every object in the Pics de Sandou is sacred. You took this object. It will kill you. You must return it. Now."

Geordie managed to groan, "Take it, then. Take it back."

"No, monsieur, you took it. You offended the gods. You must seek pardon from a *féticheur* to lift the spell. You must take it back tonight or you will die."

Geordie managed a "Yeah, right" expression with his eyes. He had never heard such codswallop. He'd simply caught a tropical fever. Coming to think of it he'd forgotten to take his Doxycyclene anti-malarial pills for the past few days. A mosquito could have infected him. He hated the hysteria over animism in this primitive country.

"I fear this *féticheur*. Tonight we go back. Take a shower and dress. We go back now, Geordie." Kaya helped him to his feet. Geordie's legs were rubbery and his head was spinning, but he managed to stand under a cold shower and clear his pores of dirt and sweat. He pulled on his shorts and a tee shirt, slipped into loafers and crashed out of the door. Kaya helped him into the car. The piece of pottery rattled in the ashtray in the arm rest.

"*Ce truc commence à devenir mal* – this thing's starting to get evil," Kaya exclaimed. The streets of Bobo Dioulasso were empty as they raced out of town towards Banfora. It was two in the morning. There were no street lights. The car's main beam caught the eyes of a dog slinking in the gutter and a family of piglets foraging in garbage on the roadside.

Geordie sat expressionless in the passenger seat, staring at the waning moon as it flitted between the trees. He felt disembodied, detached from the events he was caught up in. A headache pulsed behind his eyes. He could barely lift his arm to scratch his face. He began to gasp for air, his head lolled. The villages were quiet, resting darkly in the tranquillity of the night as the car sped along the road. He rasped to Kaya, "Open the window." He felt the billowing humid air in his face as he retched into the night, then slumped back in his seat. "*Merci*," he said quietly, closing his eyes.

Kaya watched his friend with considerable alarm. They reached Banfora at four in the morning. The Pics de Sandou were still an hour away. Where would he find the *féticheur* Moka at five in the morning? He might be in any one of eight villages within a 10-mile radius. Time was draining away. Geordie was slumped in his seat, cadaverously pale, breathing irregularly. Kaya shook him to keep him alert, but he didn't respond. He was unconscious, not asleep.

THE SHARD OF POTTERY

When they reached Voulu Zonga, Kaya drove roughly onto a verge and stopped. He grabbed the pottery and ran up the track towards the village. He knew it was a terrible risk because strangers wandering around remote African villages at night might easily be killed. Fair game: nobody entering a village at that hour could be presumed innocent. When he reached the gate he ran towards a hut where the embers of a fire still glowed in a metal grate outside the door. He stooped to peer into the dark doorway. Someone must still be awake, surely?

"*Il-y-a quelqu'un?*" he called. Silence. Kaya stood up and turned. Two huge shadowy figures loomed immediately behind him, outlined by the moon's faint light. Their height was enhanced by hideous masks. They carried heavy knobbed sticks. Kaya jumped. He put up his hands to show he was unarmed. "There's an emergency. I need to see the *sorcier*. A man is dying." Kaya was grabbed and pulled further into the village. He was thrown onto the ground in front of a hut. The men thumped the earth hard with their sticks. A small figure emerged from the shadows. "My name is Kaya. I saw you yesterday when my client wanted to take a photograph of Voulu Zonga. Now he is very sick. I need your help."

A young woman came out of the hut and lit a fire. When the *sorcier* saw Kaya he waved away the two masked men. They stepped back a few paces. The *sorcier* was completely naked, a skeletal old man with tightly curled grey hair. Kaya handed him the piece of pottery. He shrieked and threw it to the ground. He danced around it, poked it, kicked it, screamed at it, stomped on it, ranted, rolled his eyeballs and, with a primal scream that would waken the dead, grabbed a stick from one of the masked men and thumped the shard of pottery to dust. He stood over the spot for ten minutes with his head bowed, jerking and muttering incantations, then stood straight and walked across to Kaya,

"That will be 5000 francs."

Kaya fished into his pocket and gave the sorcier a note for 10,000. "*Merci, seigneur.*"

The old man grinned toothlessly. "*Je te donne du bon grigri.*"

Dawn was spreading its light across the eastern horizon by the time Kaya returned to the vehicle.

"Where the hell have you been?" Geordie was standing outside the car.

"I had to see a friend." Kaya patted Geordie on the shoulder. "Get in. We need to find some coffee and drive back to Bobo Dioulasso. We have a lot to talk about."

Chapter 4

Poisonous Old Git

"Do you know what Winston Churchill's definition of success was?"

It was a strange question to be asked as an opening gambit by a stranger. Geordie was nodding to sleep against the dirty glass of the window as the train sped through darkening Kentish countryside.

Geordie looked up at the man across the aisle. He was dressed in well-tailored but threadbare clothes. His navy blazer was a good 30 years old, as were his twill slacks, polished black brogues, starched shirt and the faded club tie which Geordie recognized but couldn't identify. He had a fine accent, spoken in that rakish world-weary tone which many women, and most Americans, generally found devastatingly attractive. He hadn't shaved that day and seemed rather flyblown.

"I'm sure I know, at least I knew . . . er . . . it wouldn't be hard to construct a definition of success that would fit Winston Churchill's view of the world," Geordie fumbled back.

"Winston Churchill's definition of success was 'Going from failure to failure without loss of enthusiasm.'"

Geordie laughed, replying with a slightly patronizing "Nice one." He wasn't in the mood to converse on the train. He was tired and rather hoped to be left alone until he reached Dover Priory.

"I've thought about it for a long time," the chap continued, "It's a nice definition on principle, but it was all right for him to say that, wasn't it? He messed up his school career at Harrow, but at least he had the opportunity to go there and mess it up, didn't he?"

"You could say that," Geordie replied cautiously.

"He had multiple failures all the way to Downing Street, but at least he was politically connected enough to have the opportunity to fail. If your father's Randolph Churchill and your mother's an American heiress, if your great, great, great grandfather was the Duke of Marlborough and you were born in Blenheim Palace, it does rather give you the confidence to go from failure to failure without loss of enthusiasm, doesn't it?"

"Well, yes, I suppose it does. But it's still not a bad attitude to govern your life by, is it?"

"I think it's a do-good churchy way to go about your life. It's the privileged application of Turn the Other Cheek. Think about it – if a bully does you over and you offer him the other cheek, it'll give him even more pleasure to whack you again. That's what bullies are. They love weaklings."

Geordie was starting to dislike this man. Being interrupted from his slumbers was one thing, being interrupted with an earful of bitterness was really too much. It seemed odd that such an officer-like fellow should harbour so much bile. He didn't look like one of the world's natural victims.

"As life has gone by I've stopped forgiving people. That's what people want – to be forgiven. If you forgive them they can then go and mess up other peoples' lives with a clean conscience."

"But bitterness will corrode you more than any person you hate," Geordie took issue. "If you forgive people, you put all your anger behind you."

"If you lash out immediately, then you can make amends and forget." The chap smirked. "You don't have to waste energy forgiving people. You've got your revenge. That's the best way."

"That's a matter of opinion. Revenge just feeds on itself. If you forgive someone the spirit of revenge fizzles out." Geordie wanted to wind down this conversation. He was tired after a long day. Besides, he was conscious of fellow passengers taking an interest in what was being said. He didn't want to be associated with this man.

He ignored Geordie's views on forgiveness. "You sometimes just have to take your time and pace yourself. An opportunity will nearly always present itself. I like the American attitude to forgiveness – Don't get mad, get even. If you're slighted by someone and you can't immediately get a remedy, take your time and one day, when they least expect it, you'll have the perfect opportunity to get revenge. What goes around, comes around."

Geordie hated that cliché. "That's one way to approach life, I suppose. But it's not my style. I prefer to forgive and forget. I prefer another American adage – Love your enemies, they'll hate you for it."

"Corny but useless. Have you any idea how much contempt is heaped on people like that?"

"If that's your attitude, you lose mental hygiene," Geordie said wearily. "Can you honestly give an example of when you got even with someone and felt better as a result?"

"Good Lord, yes." The man's face creased into a David Niven smile. "A few years ago I was in Barbados on holiday. I met a lady by the pool who seemed a cut above the others. After spending an afternoon with her I realized she was the wife of my boss at the law firm where I worked."

"No names?" Geordie asked out of tabloid curiosity.

"Emphatically no names. Her husband caused me years of misery as he bypassed me for promotion as a young man. I worked hard and was always pressured to produce more, which I did. He always took the credit for my work. He was afraid to promote me in case his bluff was called. One year at appraisal time, I was given a 5 per cent pay rise when the rate of inflation was 12 per cent. I went to his office after opening the pay envelope. I told him that my pay rise was well below the inflation rate and that to live in London I needed a proper increase. My boss looked at me in astonishment, remarking, "My dear fellow, if you need cash to tide you over, why don't you just sell some shares?" The man laughed with a whinny like a horse. "As if everybody owned so many shares that their salary for working was just by the by."

"Quite so."

"I took his wife out to dinner and squired her for the rest of my holiday in Barbados. She didn't have a clue that her husband was my boss or that I knew anything about her background. I never let on."

"Sounds like you got pretty even on that occasion. But what about her? Weren't you just deceiving an innocent woman?"

"Innocent?" the man sneered. "The funny thing was that when I left my boss's room after my discussion I knew that an opportunity would present itself sometime in the future. I didn't know how, what, where or when, but I knew it would. And it did, with interest."

"Do you have other examples?"

"Dozens. I keep a file of people who have caused me grief over the years. I've repaid most of them one way or another. Mind you, I never go looking for revenge. It just presents itself. As soon as someone thinks they've got rid of me, I have a knack of cropping up in a situation where I hold the trump card."

"Do you ever get the same person twice?"

"No, that would be vindictive. Once is enough. If you kick someone once in the balls at least as hard as he kicked you, that's enough. Beyond that, revenge can get obsessive. Not that I haven't hit someone back more than once from time to time, mind you, but the real pleasure is in the first surprise."

"So, your file? How long do you keep it for?"

"As long as it takes. There are some people I will never be able to repay. Some live in totally different parts of the world. One chap wrote me a long letter from Bristol at Christmas one year. It said that

I had been on his conscience for years and asked if I would please accept his Christmas greetings as a symbol of reconciliation."

"That was nice of him."

"Was it hell! The bastard thought he could atone for years of bullshit on his part by sending a cheery Christmas card."

"Did you respond?"

"Very much so. I was much older, of course. As luck would have it, by then I'd become a trustee of his pension fund. I introduced a motion to reduce some of his entitlements 'for actuarial reasons'. For the greater good of the long-term beneficiaries of the fund, you understand. He began to suffer financially. He never knew that I had any influence over his affairs. Still doesn't. He just sees his situation as a misfortune."

"Anybody else?"

"Unfortunately a few have died before I could repay them. They never got to know what life's whiplash felt like."

"I'd have thought that dying would be whiplash enough, from your standpoint."

"Not really. They died surrounded by their loved ones. I was robbed of their astonishment when they realized I had trumped them."

The train began to brake as it approached Folkestone.

"Well, this is my stop. I thoroughly enjoyed talking to you. I hope you enjoy the rest of your journey." He slid a wallet from his breast pocket and pulled out a copper-engraved card. It bore the name of a well-known financier from the 1980s.

Geordie took the card and replied, "I'm sorry I don't have any cards on me."

"If you ever want to have lunch in the City or discuss a career in the upper reaches of finance, please don't hesitate to give me a call." He whipped a battered attaché case from the rack above his seat and made his way along the aisle towards the door. He didn't look back as he alighted from the train and walked with a smile on his face along the platform past Geordie's window.

A fat woman had sat quietly opposite Geordie throughout their conversation. As soon as the gentleman was out of earshot, she remarked loudly in a Canvey Island accent, "Upper reaches of foinance, my arse. Wot a poisonous old git."

Several other passengers nodded. Geordie closed his eyes. He couldn't help reflecting on the man's take on Winston Churchill's definition of success. It was a great mechanism to persuade oneself not to go mad after a string of failures, for sure. But this bloke was not living by it. Quite the opposite. He was a vindictive old codger ticking off his enemies, real or imagined, one by one. What a dreadful way to spend his retirement. He smiled to himself; the fat woman's right. Wot a poisonous old git.

Chapter 5

Café de la Paix

He shook his housemaster's hand for the last time.

"You'll always have a home here, Kinloch. And remember, whenever you get into a tight spot in life, old chap, *plus est en vous.*"

Geordie couldn't help feeling sorry for his corduroyed, balding housemaster. It must be sad to nurture generations of schoolboys into manhood, only to see them disappear into the Big Wide World and, largely, never hear from them again.

"Thank you sir, not to mention *Odi et amo, mea Clodia.*"

"Cheeky bugger. Off you go now, it's time. Be careful in the BWW." The housemaster's facial muscles tensed as Geordie loaded his trunk and guitar cases into the guard's van.

Geordie clambered onto the train. Doors banged, a whistle blew and five years slid into history. The school had successfully delivered another well-rounded young man into the world. He was primed to play rugby, serve the community and share Catullus with passing strangers. He knew no girls of his own age but had supreme confidence that he would meet one soon and fall in love.

Steeped in the qualities of a hearty Edwardian education, Geordie sat back, stared at the passing fields and summed up what he knew about the fast-moving world of 1968. For all his drilling in the ancient Classics, sports, social skills and precocious knowledge, the answer, he concluded, was fuck all.

He inhaled the fragrant August breeze through his studio window. As his eyes roved across the rooftops they homed in on the leggy brunette in the apartment opposite. Her hair was tied into a springy pony tail as she vacuumed her bedroom in the sunshine, quite naked, teasingly oblivious to the wide-eyed stare she attracted from her neighbour. Usually she commanded his interest absolutely, but not today. Geordie's lungs tingled and his head was giddy from the warm summer wind blowing off the lake. Adrenalin made his heart spike with excitement. His total existence for the past month, for his entire life coming to that, was focused on this very day. He was almost sick with anticipation and apprehension. He was going to see Mireille again that afternoon.

They'd arranged to meet after lunch. He had six hours to kill. He flicked through a pile of LPs, carefully removed one from its sleeve and placed it on the rubber mat on his turntable. He stripped, filled the basin and soaped his face to the bluesy grit of Creedence Clearwater Revival. He shaved meticulously, paying close regard to squaring his youthful sideburns and smoothing the stubble around his nose and mouth. To the strains of '*Proud Mary*' he stood in the shower, shampooed and soaped himself . . . You don't know . . . the good side of a city . . . till you hitch a ride on a riverboat queen . . . Geordie calmed his nerves by singing along to this anthem of an easy-going hippie lifestyle. He would dearly love the experience of travelling on a Mississippi riverboat and have something real to talk about.

He slapped Eau Sauvage on his face. Today he would wear his best shirt, his tapered white Swiss cotton chemise with a faintly embroidered edelweiss on the front, bought for a friend's wedding a month ago. He would wear his grey Glen Urquhart check suit and polished silver-buckled Bally shoes. No tie. He emulated the casual playboy look that he'd seen at the IOS Club in Ferney Voltaire. How he admired those hot young American mutual fund salesmen in their scarlet Porsche Targas, racing up to Gstaad at weekends with their coltish girlfriends.

Geordie took one last look in the mirror and clicked the studio door firmly behind him. He stepped out of the building into the sunshine and turned left down Rue Rothschild. Along the lake he headed towards the Pont du Mont Blanc. Stylish couples promenaded with their dogs and children, sailboats flitted across the green water, swallows screeched over the potted geraniums which festooned the discreet penthouse balconies. He was intoxicated by the seductive affluence of Geneva in high summer. How he fantasized about the delights that unfolded behind those ornate lakeside facades.

It was his turn at the booth at Cornavin, Geneva's main station.

"*Aller-retour à Lausanne, s'il vous plaît.*"

"*Aujourd'hui seulement?*"

"*Je reviendrai demain.*" Of course he would stay the night.

He caught a whiff of cheap cigar smoke as the tickets slid through the opening.

"*Merci.*"

It was 1.30 p.m. Mireille would meet him in exactly one hour outside the Buffet de La Gare in Lausanne. Floating in magic, he found his platform and stood under the clock. Seven minutes to departure. How he longed to be with her. He hated to squander one second of time away from the love of his life.

The train slid out of Cornavin and soon left Geneva far behind. Geordie watched the terraced vineyards race by, tucked into the southern foothills of the Jura. He wondered who lived in the chateaux, who was in the picturesque paddle steamers criss-crossing Lake Geneva, what went on in the tree-screened lakeside estates of the über-rich. The train stopped at Nyon, then at Rolle, again at Morges. Lausanne was next. Geordie went to the toilet for a final check. He combed his hair, rinsed his mouth – *eau non potable* – straightened his jacket and waited in the corridor as the train slowed.

2.20 p.m. He stepped off the carriage onto the hallowed concrete of Lausanne station. As Geordie made his way through the crowds he spotted her. She was absently turning a postcard carousel outside a newsagent stall in the concourse. Her feet were bare, her shiny black hair fell in rich ringlets down her back. She wore a cream blouse and a pale green skirt. No bra, as usual. A brightly coloured Moroccan hessian bag was draped over her bare shoulder.

"Mireille?" he sidled up to her without being seen.

"*Oui?*" she replied abstractedly. Geordie moved forward to kiss her mouth but she reflexively turned her head so he only kissed her cheek.

"You look lovely, Mireille."

"Thank you."

"Are you all right? You seem preoccupied."

"No, I'm fine."

"I've missed you enormously."

"Have you?" she asked in a flat, mildly surprised tone.

"It's been a month since we saw each other."

"Has it?"

Something terrible was happening. Geordie panicked. The effervescent chemistry that pulsed between them a month earlier had gone.

"Shall we look around Lausanne?" Geordie suggested limply. He tried to slip his arm around her waist but she sidestepped deftly; she only let him hold her hand. His mouth turned as dry as a cake. They headed uphill into the Old Town. Despite a month of excited chatter bottled up in him, he had nothing to say but fatuous observations about Lausanne's street life as it unfolded.

They walked on cobbled roads and encountered a troupe of African street dancers. Their black muscular bodies were semi-naked, gyrating to the voodoo rhythm of tom toms on the pavement outside a café. Mireille was amused by the animal energy of the dancers and she seemed to thaw, but Geordie felt inert and Presbyterian among the contorting bodies.

It began to rain. They ducked into the cathedral where Mireille showed him the stained glass. They explored a chapel. As they stood beside a group of medieval carvings a peal of thunder cracked above them. Rain cascaded against the windows. Mireille's hair was wet. Geordie's face moved towards hers. She turned her head.

"What's wrong, Mireille?"

"Nothing."

"Something's changed." He held both her hands and looked imploringly into her face.

"You mustn't love me."

"The sun mustn't rise." Geordie tried to kiss her again. She turned away.

"I belong to someone else."

Geordie felt as if he'd been stabbed.

"Why . . . didn't you say so earlier?"

"Because I wanted to see you."

"Why, so that you could kick me in person?"

"It's not like that. I really like you."

"So who do you belong to, then?" Geordie was crushed but at least it was a relief to break the tension.

"He lives in Milan."

"Oh God, not another Luigi." Geordie recalled a recent conversation with a German girl about the irresistibility of Italians.

"He's Ukrainian," she replied defensively, ". . . originally."

"Oh. What's his name?"

"Dimitri."

"How long have you known him?"

"Three years."

"Why didn't you say anything when we first met?" he asked imploringly. "Didn't London mean anything to you?"

"I loved being with you in London. I sort of forgot him when I first met you. He was on National Service in Italy. He hadn't written or called me for a month. I didn't think he cared anyway. I thought it was over." Geordie's heart sank further when he realized she was speaking in the past tense.

He recalled the cosmic excitement of that steamy July day in Hyde Park. Mick Jagger released a cloud of butterflies and recited lines from Shelley's Adonais in honour of the dead Stones' guitarist Brian Jones. London was the epicentre of the universe. Geordie had been crazed with love, lying on the grass with his sensuous French girlfriend. Nightingales had sung in the chambers of his heart. Mireille and he had been totally, like, Where It's At. If that day could have been transposed into eternity, he would have attained Nirvana; his universal spiritual mission already accomplished at the age of 18.

"As we lay together in Hyde Park, you were thinking of Dimitri?"

"I was completely with you in London." Mireille hung her head, staring at her feet. "Dimitri was on military service. As I said to you, I hadn't heard from him for ages. I thought it was over."

"But it's not . . ."

"I told him about you. He said he loved me. I told him the best way to show his love was to leave me alone."

"I think we should go for a drink."

The clouds were clearing as they walked out of the cathedral. Beams of sunlight sparkled off the wet pavements. Mireille held his hand more firmly than earlier. They were both relieved to have broken the ice. She wordlessly led him downhill in the direction of the station.

"Here's a place," Mireille suggested, "let's go inside." They entered a smoky bistro, the Café de la Paix. They squeezed past a knot of drinkers standing in front of a television and sat at a corner table by the window. As they took their seats she tossed her mane of hair and smiled unexpectedly. She looked relaxed for the first time that afternoon. Geordie touched her hand across the table. "What was that about?"

"Nothing. I can smile, can't I?"

Emboldened, Geordie leaned across the table and held her hand. As limp as a fish again. His heart sank. "What do you want to drink?"

"Pastis." She looked down at her hands; they were fidgeting with a pack of Gauloises.

"Sounds like a good idea." He ordered the drinks. "So, you told him to leave you alone?"

"Sort of."

"And you told him about me?"

"Yes. I told him. He's very jealous."

Misery . . . the present tense again.

"I suppose that's a good sign. You must have expressed enough feelings about me for him to take me seriously."

"I do like you. Here . . ." She handed him the cigarettes. He slid an untipped Gauloise into his hand, perched it drily on his lower lip, flipped open his Zippo and lit up in a practised gesture. He'd seen Marlon Brando light up in a similar way. The waiter busily delivered two glasses of pastis to their table, together with a jug. Geordie splashed water into the clear pastis, which instantly clouded. He drew smoke through his nostrils and blew it into the air above his head.

"Santé." He clinked her glass.

"Santé."

"But I'm crazy about you. We were made for each other."

"Maybe in another world, another time, but I belong to Dimitri."

"Do you love him?"

"He's got something."

"And I haven't?"

"Yes . . . ," she hesitated, "but you're very different from him."

"What about our time together in London? The concert in Hyde

Park. Lying in the shade, holding each other tight." He repeated the question disbelievingly. "Didn't that mean anything to you?"

"It was lovely." They were silent for a few moments. Geordie took hope from her words but his world was evaporating.

"Do . . . do you . . . you know . . . with Dimitri?"

"Make love?"

"Yes. I suppose that's it. Do you make love with him?"

"Sometimes." She looked sideways away from Geordie and smiled again.

"What about us?"

"I want to be your friend."

"I don't know how to be your friend after what we've done together. We're lovers, we have to be lovers. I'm your lover, Mireille. We were meant for each other. It's in the stars."

"I belong to Dimitri, Geordie." She looked down at her hands, adding quietly, "He said he would kill himself if I left him."

Something about his stoical British schooling prevented Geordie from pulling the same stunt. A volatile Slav might frighten a girl into pledging her heart by threatening suicide, but Geordie could never behave like that. He looked desperately into those blue eyes, her pale oval face framed by coal-black gypsy hair. He worshipped every part of her, every stitch of her clothes down to her blackened hippie feet. But for all their preordained cosmic twinning, she had, quite simply, gone cold on him.

Geordie downed the remaining pastis from his glass and signalled to the waiter. "*L'addition, s'il vous plaît.*" His heart was breaking but he had to appear in control, normal, unaffected. Turning back to Mireille, in the most casual tone he could muster, he told her, "I have to get back to Geneva. I have some plans this evening." He lied, hoping to raise the tiniest spark of jealousy in her. There was none, not even polite curiosity. He paid.

As they left the café Mireille smiled the same smile as when they had entered an hour earlier. She took Geordie's hand firmly, "I'll come with you to the station."

Geordie found himself walking extremely slowly. He desperately wanted to spin out his remaining precious moments with her.

"Tell me about Dimitri."

"His mother is wonderful. She adores me. He lives partly in Milan . . ." she tapered off.

"And partly . . . ?"

Mireille looked at her feet again. That diffidence! Geordie worshipped her. There was so much he could do for her, if only she would allow him.

". . . And partly in Switzerland." She was sensitive enough not to say 'with me.' But that is what she meant, although he desperately wanted to ignore the hint.

"I'd like to meet him sometime," he said bravely.

"He wouldn't be nice to you. You're so different."

"I'd still like to meet him sometime."

"You already have . . ."

Geordie looked blank.

"Sort of . . ." she added, smiling again in the way she had smiled in the café.

"What do you mean?"

"I told him I wanted to be alone with you today but he followed me to the station and walked behind us."

"He was watching us all afternoon? Was he in the cathedral?"

"No. But he was sitting at the table next to us in the café. His mother owns the Café de la Paix."

Geordie stopped momentarily on the pavement. All he could say, very quietly, was, "I see."

After a few paces, he turned to Mireille. "Don't bother to come any further. I can find the station." He pecked her on both cheeks, French style. Her eyes welled with tears. Geordie turned and walked down the hill, leaving her standing on the pavement. He couldn't bear to look back.

He sat in the train, utterly immobile, staring blankly into the middle distance of vineyards and sailboats. He handed his ticket to the collector automatically, without looking at the man. He thought of the words *Plus est en vous*, mustering a wry smile in recognition of the innocent optimism they represented. On arrival in Geneva he walked very slowly from the station down the Rue du Mont Blanc and meandered along the lake promenade. Couples laughed and played on restaurant terraces by the shore. The same menu sign was propped against the wall, exactly where he'd eaten with Mireille six weeks ago: *Perche du Lac – Specialité de la Maison*.

He walked for several miles along the promenade and leaned on a limestone block by the lapping water. The Pointillist pink and turquoise dusk faded into the blackest night over the lake. He gazed at the lights twinkling happily on the plane trees across in Eaux Vives. Paddleboats glided majestically towards the far shore as laughing lovers enjoyed the strains of Strauss waltzes while they dined on board. Wine glasses clinked over the calm water.

Geordie was invited to address a conference in Lausanne. It was an annual boondoggle for the benefit of the institutional clients of an American bank. The flight from London arrived in Geneva in the early afternoon. He boarded the train directly from the airport and sped along the lakeside corridor. Not much countryside remained from his distant recollections of over two decades ago. Sprawling developments dominated the lake shore, vineyards were now squeezed between high-rise apartments; concrete and cranes infested the landscape. The flowery meadows of his youth and the crystal views of the French Alps had been supplanted by toxic highways and a sulphurous pall obscuring Mont Blanc.

The train drew into Lausanne. He was not expected at the Beau Rivage for a few hours. His bag was light and he welcomed the chance to stretch his legs in the sunshine. He made his way uphill towards the Old Town. In the backstreets a group of young Africans had set out stalls in the sunshine. Rows of black wooden Makonde carvings were displayed on woven rugs on the pavement. As he wondered who in Lausanne might buy such tacky African ornaments he looked up and spotted the sign: Café de la Paix.

"I don't believe it, I wonder if. . . ." Geordie instinctively crossed the road and entered the tired-looking bistro. It was empty but for an unshaven afternoon boozer staring into space, enveloped in a cloud of blue smoke from a cigarillo. Geordie took a seat by the window.

"*Vous désirez?*" the grizzled barman barked at him in a thick accent.

"*Pastis, s'il vous plaît.*"

Geordie tipped water into his glass. He never failed to enjoy a childlike delight when the clear pastis turned cloudy. He savoured its strong medicinal flavour. It evoked hissing cicadas, azure waves and, as it turned out, wildly unfulfilled hopes on the French Riviera in his distant past.

He surveyed the interior of the café. Rows of dusty liqueur bottles along a glass shelf, a missing lightbulb, worn linoleum, cigarette burns on the bar surface, streaked windows, an uncleared table. A TV at the far end of the bar showed two obscure Swiss football teams playing to a frenzied commentary. He wondered if it was the same place. Twenty-five years had passed. He tried, but could match nothing in the café to the abruptly revived memories of that distant day.

He paid and slung his bag over his shoulder for the final stretch to the Beau Rivage. As he left the café a young girl in a wheelchair pushed past him at the door. She was followed by a thin, tired-looking woman, her lank hair streaked with grey. Her face was furrowed and her complexion sallow.

As they passed in the doorway their eyes met for an instant. She looked towards the barman, then glanced back quizzically at Geordie. Puzzled, she shook her head faintly. He said nothing. He was incognito, a random stranger passing through the café, a lifetime out of context. She smiled awkwardly; he looked through her and stepped into the sunshine.

He floated through the leafy warm streets of Lausanne and checked into the Beau Rivage. Later, at a magnificent reception for the financial conference, he turned down a flute of vintage champagne and asked the waitress for a glass of pastis. The banking delegates were gathered on the terrasse with a magnificent view of Lac Leman. Turbocharged financial chatter wafted around him but Geordie stood aloof. He stared out at the Impressionistic colours on the water as the sun dipped over the Jura. *Plus est en vous?* Not this time, he reflected.

Chapter 6

San Andreas

"Matthew Chance speaking."

"Geordie Kinloch here."

"Geordie Kinloch? Good God, there's a name from the past! Where on earth are you calling from?" Matthew's Sandhurst vowels were still clipped after 20 years of California living. Geordie envisaged his old friend in the morning sunshine on a dappled veranda commanding a view of a vineyard in Napa Valley.

"I'm in New York right now. I got your number from Dan in your old office. He said you wouldn't mind if I got in touch. The reason I'm calling is that I've got some meetings in San Francisco next Monday, the 19th. I was wondering if you were free for lunch or dinner sometime over the weekend? Haven't seen you for years. It would be great to catch up."

"That would be nice. Problem is, we live a long way out of town in Marin. What with the dogs and horses, it's hard to get into town at short notice."

"Not to worry if you can't fit it in. I just don't see myself returning to the Coast for a while. I thought it might be fun to catch up while we were both in the same time zone."

Matthew took the bait. "It might be easier for you to visit us out here. Why don't you come out and stay?"

"That would be great, but I wouldn't want to impose myself on you and your family." Matthew was a private fellow. He was now out of the finance scene but not long ago he was one of the few names quoted reverentially in the Wall Street press. Perhaps he didn't want to be reminded of those days.

"Not at all. The kids are off our hands and living away. Things are fairly quiet next weekend. Why don't you just come down after lunch on Saturday? We'll have a good dinner, you can stay the night, have a leisurely start in the morning and head back to the city on Sunday afternoon. We can shoot the breeze over dinner and catch up. And you'll get a chance to meet Serena."

"Serena?" Geordie asked tentatively. His friend had a patchy marital record.

"You may not remember her. I think I was still married to Jill when we last met."

"Yes, you were still married to Jill." Geordie changed the subject, "So, how do I find you on Saturday?"

"We're near Point Reyes National Seashore. I'll email a map with instructions how to find us. What's your email address?"

Geordie left his office in New York City at 4 p.m. on Friday afternoon to hail a cab on Park Avenue, which was not a clever start. He eventually flagged down a limo on 42nd Street driven by a heavily stubbled Greek who blocked conversation all the way to the airport. He took every short cut but got jammed in the Friday evening traffic on the way to La Guardia. As they rolled into the airport 90 minutes later, the Greek took his $80 and came out with a maddening observation: "Our culture needs less Plato and more Aristotle."

"I wish you'd said that an hour ago. We might have had an interesting discussion."

The man shrugged, muttered 'whatever' in a thick accent and sped off.

The check-in and security process seemed to drag on forever. Geordie got to the gate just in time for immediate boarding at 7.15 p.m. It was a no-frills flight. No meals, no drink. He didn't have time to purchase food in the concourse so he boarded empty-handed. There was an irritable bastard in the seat straight in front of him. The guy was in an exit row with great legroom, yet pushed his seat back almost into Geordie's lap. He could barely deploy a newspaper. The plane pulled away from the gate then sat on the tarmac until 9 p.m. The flight landed in San Francisco in turbulence and heavy rain at 11 p.m. local time — it was 2 a.m. in New York.

Geordie woke slowly, stretched and took his time. It was the first morning in weeks that he wasn't wrenched out of bed by a pre-dawn alarm call, forced to shave his tired face and bolt on a pinstripe suit in preparation for the day's financial jousting. It was Saturday. He was in a Marriott overlooking the lagoon across from San Francisco Airport. He'd driven here in a lashing rainstorm very late the previous night in a rental car, getting drenched as he bolted to the hotel's reception. The restaurant was closed. He checked into the hotel wet, knackered, hungry and bad-tempered.

There was one objective today, which was to roll up at the Chance residence in Marin County 'sometime after lunch'. The luxury of time was intoxicating. He had seven hours to get up, potter over the Golden Gate Bridge, turn north on Route One, mosey up the coast, stroll on a beach, perhaps get spindrift in his hair. . . . He wondered what Matthew Chance's place was like. He imagined an immaculately maintained ranch, shiny racehorses grazing behind white fences. He imagined immaculately white-coated Mexicans padding around the hot-tub dispensing pina coladas to the guests.

Matthew had once worked as the global lending director of a multinational bank with tens of billions under his control. In his late 30s he broke off to start his own financial consultancy in San Francisco. He became a financial pioneer in Brazil, Korea and India when those countries were considered completely off-limits by any credit control officer who valued his career in conventional banking. His consultancy was a success and he sold it well after 10 years.

After the sale he took time off to travel around the globe. Teaming up with different friends on various legs of his travels, Matthew had hiked the Atlas Mountains in Morocco, explored the South Pacific in a catamaran, fished mountain rivers in Southern Chile, ridden across the Mongolian plains, sailed around Tierra del Fuego and biked a wild section of the Rift Valley. He had treated himself to a global whirlwind of adventures, then disappeared into the hedonistic backwoods of Marin County in California.

Geordie looked forward to seeing how Matthew had reinvented himself. His own career wasn't far behind. Quite soon he'd like to take a similar leap and retreat to the family pile in the Scottish Highlands.

After breakfast Geordie checked out and tossed his bag into the back of the car. He drove north through San Francisco and out across the Golden Gate Bridge. Its massive riveted rusty-hued towers melted into the mist hundreds of feet above the cars. It was a clammy morning. He recalled the gruesome statistic that the bridge had averaged one suicide every 15 days since its completion in 1937.

The bodies were generally sucked out to sea or became lunch to marauding sharks. One guy apparently jumped off and survived. He swam disconsolately to shore and announced to the startled bystanders, "I didn't even get that right." Geordie wondered why the authorities didn't leave up the safety net installed for the construction workers. It had saved the lives of 19 men as they plummeted out of the sky during the bridge's construction. They called themselves the 'Halfway to Hell Club'.

On the far side he turned north along Route One. After a stretch of malls and suburbia the road became rustic. It meandered uphill through cypress and eucalyptus groves, around ravines and gulches. A few miles further on it opened into a panoramic view of the Pacific Ocean at the John Muir Park Outlook. Geordie stopped at the deserted beauty spot. Warnings against rip tides and great white sharks were posted on notice boards in the car park. He stood on a Second World War gun emplacement, marvelling at the curve of the beach disappearing along the Pacific into a distant infinity of spume and mist. He took an enormous breath and opened his arms to the onshore wind. A formation of pelicans flew by.

He continued driving northwards. Route One was carved out of unstable, friable cliffs where a road really didn't belong. It was indented with landslides, both from the cliffs above and from sections of tarmac sliding into oblivion below. The road surface was buckled in many places, presumably by a combination of flash floods, braking trucks, extreme temperatures and periodic earthquakes.

Geordie reached Stinson Beach at 11 a.m. He was only half an hour's drive from his destination near Point Reyes Station and was not expected for hours. He parked and strolled along the main drag, bought a vegetarian pitta sandwich at an organic grocery store and found a bench overlooking the beach. A middle-aged hippie sat at the far end of the same bench, reading *The Wall Street Journal*.

"Mind if I sit down?"

"Hell, no! Be my guest." The guy wore an old denim shirt, jeans and cowboy boots. His luxuriant grey hair was swept into a tight pony-tail held back with a rubber band.

"Thanks." Geordie sat and unwrapped his sandwich.

"Where you from, buddy?" The man closed his paper.

"Scotland. How about you?" Geordie batted the conversation back. He didn't particularly feel like explaining himself to a stranger.

"I'm a Scotsman too. My grandparents came from Paisley." The guy replied in a lilting Californian accent, "Jack's my name. I'm a musician and I live right here in Stinson Beach."

"What instruments do you play?"

"Acoustic and electric guitar, drums, mandolin, banjo, violin, harmonica..."

"You sound like a one-man bluegrass band."

"Yea, kinda," he laughed.

"Is there enough work around Stinson Beach to keep you going?" Geordie looked over his shoulder. There weren't many houses in the village.

"Sure – if you want it. Yea, I play as a full band member sometimes, as a session musician other times." He paused and looked out to sea. "It got a whole lot quieter when Jerry died," Jack answered wistfully.

"Jerry?"

"Yea – Jerry Garcia. He used to live 'round here. A few years back the place was rocking. We got busted a few times. Cops in those days never left us alone. We all did time for possession. But man, it was a hot scene in Stinson Beach."

"How long ago was that?"

"Oh, 1967 through 1972, mebbe."

"Anything happen since then?"

"Sure, Steve Miller hung out here. He was one hell of a blues guitarist. Did you get him in Scotland?"

"Of course. But I never saw him personally."

"Yea, a lotta musicians hung out at Stinson Beach back then," Jack reminisced, "We played gigs in the Bay Area in the sixties and seventies. We crashed in Haight Ashbury. We wore crazy clothes. They were unique times, with Vietnam and Civil Rights and all that shit. That was ugly, man. We were fighting the machine. What about you guys over the pond?"

"I was young back then – We had songs like 'Waterloo Sunset', 'All You Need is Love', 'Whiter Shade of Pale'. We didn't have Vietnam but we listened to West Coast bands like the Doors and the Byrds, Country Joe and the Fish . . . "

"Country Joe! You got Country Joe in Scotland?"

"I had American friends who had his records."

They sat quietly looking at the ocean. "What's Stinson Beach famous for today?" Geordie asked.

"Like, what's Stratford-upon-Avon famous for today? We got Jerry Garcia."

"Good point, I suppose."

"But things are real quiet these days," Jack admitted ruefully, "It's peaceful here, nice beach-houses, good people, bikers, tourists, that kinda thing." Geordie stuffed the last piece of pitta bread sandwich into his mouth.

"Well, I'd better get a move on. I have to meet some people along the coast this afternoon. Great to meet you, Jack." Geordie held out his hand, "I'll let you get on with your *Wall Street Journal*."

"Yea – good to meet you, man. Enjoy your time in the Peace Zone."

Geordie walked back into the village from the ocean and made his way uphill to take a look around. The houses were modest, the sort of places inhabited by hippie aunts who never quite left the 1960s. Wind chimes, faded blue clapboard, sea shells on the windowsills, carved driftwood, old Volkswagens in driveways, the smell of sage and incense. Stinson Beach was untidy in an educated way. He felt he could easily live here.

He drove 15 miles further north and stopped to look at Matthew's instructions. He expected to be looking for a neat ranch tucked into the folds of a lush green valley, with security gates. Its address conjured up this vision – Beauregard Ranch House. He began to pass pretty houses set back from the road and Hereford cattle grazing in paddocks. He turned into a side road towards the Point Reyes National Seashore. A steady breeze off the Pacific gave the trees a permanent landward tilt.

After two miles he saw on the right a battered wooden sign for

Beauregard Ranch pointing down a rough track. He stopped, checked his instructions, shrugged and turned. The track passed through scrubby woods and ended at a dilapidated house by a muddy creek. A faded green Cadillac was parked under a tree, two bikes leaned against the porch steps. It seemed unlikely, but at least he could get out and ask for directions.

As he was parking, two enormous mastiffs crashed through the porch doors, bounded down the steps and charged towards his car in a cacophony of deep-throated barks. A familiar figure followed them. He shouted above the din, "Don't worry about them. They love people."

When Geordie opened his car door he was swamped by affectionate slobbers from the two well-meaning, if intimidating brutes. Matthew caught up with them and shook Geordie's hand. "Great to see you again. Welcome to Beauregard. Oh – meet Stanford and Oxford. They're a couple of softies, really."

"I can see that." Geordie was taken aback by the vision of Matthew. He had lost weight since they last met, he looked older and he bore no trace of the affluent sheen that accompanied his former Wall Street persona. He was dressed in old clothes but nevertheless looked fit and relaxed. He had a laid-back air that Geordie hadn't seen before in him. He only knew Matthew Chance as a driven, hard-assed banker on a mission.

"Let me help you with your luggage."

"That's OK thanks. I can carry it. I only have an overnight bag." Geordie followed him inside. It was a wooden farmhouse, maybe a century old. The hallway was sparsely furnished. It contained a scruffy chest of drawers surmounted by a cheap lamp, three stained sporting prints on the walls, a boot-rack and a side-table where car keys and pieces of mail were lying.

"Come on upstairs." Matthew led him up a flight of bare wooden steps. They emerged into a large, spacious and light room. The furniture reminded Geordie of the jumble of taste which might be found in any country house in Britain. A dark Jacobean gate-legged oak table, a Victorian mahogany glass-fronted bookcase which included, he noted with a cursory glance, Liddell Hart's History of the First World War and Siegfried Sassoon's Memoirs of an Infantry Officer. The room contained overstuffed armchairs upholstered in floral chintz, sofas in the same material, Georgian silver candlesticks and Edwardian watercolours of English rural scenes. Above the mantelpiece was an oil portrait of an 18th-century couple in front of a Georgian pile. A plaque underneath was inscribed, 'Sir Horatio Chance, Bart, and Lady Williamina Chance, Sidyates Hall, Herefordshire.'

"You might have noticed the difference between the furniture downstairs and upstairs in this house. The reason is that we're prone to flooding here. Every so often the Olema Creek rises and sweeps through the property, carrying all before it. Last time it happened at midnight on New Year's eve."

"Good lord," was all Geordie could add to the scenario.

"We were warned to expect flash flooding so the damage was minimal. We took everything from below into this room upstairs, opened the downstairs doors and windows to facilitate the current, turned off the electricity, secured the car to the big tree out there, closed its windows and hoped for the best."

"So what happened?"

"The flood duly came and rose to within six inches of this floor. That's eight feet deep, black swirling mud in the middle of the night. It was sinister, let me tell you, and bloody cold. The house became an island in a raging torrent. Not what you expect in California, is it? Serena and I stayed up, ready to jump ship. We had an inflatable boat moored to the balcony, just behind where you're standing. Just in case."

"Have you ever used it?"

"Fortunately, no. It would be touch and go getting into a small inflatable boat and floating off on a raging current down to the ocean. Particularly at night."

"Well I'll be damned. What made you move here, of all places?" Matthew laughed, "We got a very, very good deal on this house. It's uninsurable and the previous owner simply wanted rid of it at pretty much any price. Serena and I figured that if we got ten or even five years of use out of it while living in this beautiful part of Marin County, it would be worthwhile."

"That's an interesting philosophy." Geordie mused.

"Well, we've been here for eight years now and it's cost us under $500 a month to live here, all told. Have you any idea how much you'd pay to rent a 3000 square-foot, four-bedroom house in San Francisco? £6000 a month? £7000? In the meantime we've been flooded three times and lost nothing of any value."

"What about the car?"

"If you're an automobile wonk like they all are down in LA, then this place would be hell." Matthew laughed. "But we're lucky in this part of Marin County. People are anti-car and it's perfectly acceptable to tool around in an old Cadillac. After it dries out the engine starts like a dream. Let me show you your room."

Matthew crossed the drawing room to a door in the back wall. "Here you are. Why don't you get yourself organized and I'll find Serena."

Geordie was shown into a small, tidy bedroom. The single bed looked like a young girl's, with a pale green counterpane and lacy pillows. Floral curtains and a frilly table lamp completed the picture. It smelled musty, but he couldn't open the window. It was sealed, presumably to optimize the air conditioning. A private bathroom was attached to the bedroom.

He took his business suit out, hung it in the wardrobe, pulled a magnum of Moët from the bag and returned to the drawing room. Matthew and Serena stood at the far end, talking. Stanford and Oxford galumphed across the room to meet him.

"Here's a small gift for the two of you." Geordie handed Serena the bottle. She was about the same age as Matthew, slim, wiry and athletic. Her grey hair was short and trim, framing her tanned face in a latter-day Mary Quant style. Her hands were strong and practical, the hands of an outdoor person.

"Thank you so much, Geordie. We love Moët, don't we, Matty?" she smiled gracefully. "You don't mind dogs, do you?"

"Not at all – love them all," Geordie lied, patting one of the brutes on the flank. He wasn't crazy about these two. Not because they were mastiffs, but because they smelled of swamp.

"Matt tells me you were business associates many years ago. It's good to finally meet you. Welcome to Beauregard Ranch."

"Thank you, it's a pleasure to come out to Marin County and meet you too."

"Now, Geordie, if you'll excuse me, around this time in the afternoon I have to head out to the stables to feed the horses. Why don't the two of you visit together and catch up on your news? I'll be back here by six. We can have an aperitif and eat around eight, if that suits everyone?"

"That sounds wonderful, darling," Matthew replied. "I'll show Geordie around and we can have a good blather about old times."

As Serena was driving away from the house a heavy silver candlestick slid off the mantelpiece and crashed to the floor. Matthew picked it up without comment and put it back in place.

"What happened?" Geordie was startled.

"Oh, just a temblor. We get them all the time around here. You up for a walk?"

Led by the dogs, they went out into the scruffy yard. Matthew showed him the creek. It was a sluggish, shallow flow of murky water hemmed by glutinous banks of thick mud. Wading birds peep-peeped and skittered along the mud as they approached.

"It's hard to imagine this little creek rising 20 feet and raging around your house." Geordie commented.

"If there's a heavy storm in the hills to the east, the water pours straight off. It's like a storm drain. The creek can be nothing, turn into a raging torrent and back to nothing again, all in the space of three hours. The weather service is usually pretty good at warning us of storms in the hills."

"What about your neighbours?"

"None left, actually. The last one was an eccentric artist. He made ceramic pots. About three years ago he vanished in a storm with most of his house. They found some of the wreckage out in the bay. Never found his body. The site of his house was cleared and it's now reverted to the State Park system."

"Aren't you worried that the same could happen to you?"

"Not at all. We've both had great lives. It's part of the crapshoot of life."

"How very British."

"Maybe. To be honest we don't think much about it. We have wonderful, free, open lives in a beautiful part of California. What else could a couple want?"

Returning to the house, Geordie noticed crossed steel beams bracing the outside back wall. "What are they for?"

"Earthquakes."

"Earthquakes?"

"Yes, the house sits on the San Andreas Fault," he said casually.

"Bloody hell!" Geordie said involuntarily. "You mean, literally on the Fault itself? Not just like the rest of California, prone to earthquakes?

"Literally, the house straddles the San Andreas Fault. The creek follows the fault line down to Tomales Bay. You can see it clearly marked on a map. The Fault is quite narrow here and the house was built over the line."

"Bloody hell!" Geordie repeated. "So you mean to say that in an earthquake one half of the house could move south and the other could stay put?"

"Theoretically, yes. Or the fault line could overlap itself and smash the house into the size of a matchbox. We would all become part of the geological structure of Western California. During the 1906 San Francisco earthquake the biggest displacement ever recorded was on the San Andreas fault close to Point Reyes. It shifted 21 feet in some places. That's very close to here." Matthew spoke like a tour guide.

"You seem pretty cool about the prospect."

"No point worrying about it. You remember President Mitterrand's comment when he was went public with the news about his terminal cancer? He said, 'Every person in the world is on a plane journey heading straight for a mountain. The only difference between people is that most of them don't know it.'"

"Talk about living on the edge."

"Not really. Serena and I lead quiet, involved, fun-filled lives. We don't waste time worrying. If it happens, it happens. Actually, we have small temblors here practically every day. You saw the candlestick tipping off the mantelpiece earlier. That happens all the time."

"So you live on a raging flood plain straddling the San Andreas Fault?"

"Put that way, yes."

Geordie saw Matthew in a new light. He wasn't the dapper banker he remembered. He was small, wrinkled and retired; it wouldn't be hard to imagine him in a modest flat in Folkestone, shuffling around in bedroom slippers, drinking milky tea and dozing over the evening news. Yet he chose to live on top of the most notorious earthquake fault line on earth in a location prone to devastating floods, sharing his life with a sporty woman, horses and two smelly dogs.

"Well, it does seem to keep you alive, I have to admit. I always saw myself as a risk taker but my life couldn't be more boring compared to yours. In a couple of years I'll get off the treadmill and head back to Balnadarg. I'll grow trees and farm the ancestral acres. I've always known that it was there to return to and it's been a sort of insurance policy all my life."

Matthew looked at Geordie with amused condescension. "I've always avoided creating security around myself. It stifles me. This way I feel so much more free. The only stuff I own is what you see in the house. I have a few inherited items that I'm keeping for my daughter until she has a place of her own. We own the house, but it's virtually worthless. That's liberating because we don't worry about insurance, decorating or maintenance beyond keeping the place habitable. When we move, or die, or whatever, the property reverts to the State Park system. They'll bulldoze the place and plant willows on the site. After a couple of years you wouldn't know there was ever a house here."

"I suppose it must be fairly liberating after spending a career amassing wealth and financing infrastructure around the world on a grand scale."

"I don't see it like that. Once you realize how little you really need to have a great life, it's folly not to stop and enjoy yourself. Accumulating one cent beyond that point is a complete waste of your life."

"Remember Barry Brown?"

"Sure – big Irish fellow in Chicago. He ran the Tech lending desk for Kramer Bancshares. One of the best bankers of his generation. What happened to him?"

"I was at a conference 10 years ago and shared a table with him at dinner one evening. He was in his mid 50s, I'd guess. He regaled everyone with how much money was to be made in technology stock option contracts. He talked about his house on Maui, his estate in Lake Forest, his place in West Palm, his club memberships, his cars, his art, his kids at Cornell. He planned to phase into retirement with a load of non-executive board directorships. At the end of dinner he generously invited everyone at the table to visit his place in Scotland during the next British Open at St Andrews. He died of a blood clot on a plane three days later."

"I heard about that. He spent his life accumulating all that stuff, yet never got round to enjoying it. There's a lesson in there, isn't there? I bet there isn't a man alive who wouldn't trade time for stuff, if it was put to him that way."

"If you don't mind me asking, what about everything you built up over the years? Do you trade your investment account on line?"

"I set up a trust for school fees a few years ago and paid off my ex-wives with a capital sum. What was left we set up in an annuity that's enough to see us through, and maintained our health insurance. I gave up my brokerage accounts. They were too distracting. That's it." Matthew smiled.

Geordie was beginning to see more in Matthew than the old farmhouse and battered Cadillac. Granted, everything could have been tidier and better cared for, but these were simply not Matthew's priorities.

"Poor in pocket and rich in spirit. How do you spend your days?"

"Oh, we live the cycles of nature. We get up with the dawn. I love watching the birds over by the creek from the balcony. Do you realize that waders eat their own weight in molluscs and worms every day? We spend a lot of time with the dogs and horses, we ride in the morning, visit friends along the coast a few times a month. We're involved in the local community church. I read poetry and short stories. I'm co-writing a book on economic history with a PhD student at Berkeley. We go to bed early. Geordie, my man, there simply aren't enough hours in the day. I haven't even had time to take out my golf clubs this year."

After breakfast Geordie retraced Route 1 to San Francisco. He stopped at Stinson Beach to walk along the sand. His visit to Matthew Chance had been unexpectedly cathartic. He expected he would be visiting a banker's estate surrounded by high affluence and security arrangements. Instead he found a man who had cast off his baggage, leading a life of Golden Pond simplicity, with a twist.

Geordie's life accelerated away from California. After San Francisco he returned to London, followed by a week in Montreal then back to New York for two months. He seldom read non-financial newspapers and rarely watched television, so he paid scant attention to reports of El Niño playing havoc with California's weather. One Thursday morning he got a call from his friend Dan.

"Hey buddy, did you hear about Matthew?"

Geordie was watching his stock monitor, "No, what's happened?"

"He jumped out of a balloon on Sunday. No warning, bang, end of story."

"Jumped out of a balloon? What on earth was he doing in a balloon?"

"Didn't he tell you? Ballooning was one of his hobbies. He kept a couple up by the Russian River. He liked to drift over the vineyards and contemplate life. On Sunday he was out with a friend. They were 3000 feet up in a gentle breeze, he took a slug from his flask, climbed over the basket and plunged into space. He went down with a 'Yee-Ha', just like Doctor Strangelove."

"Well, I'll be damned. I saw him recently and he seemed on such good form. Did they find his body?"

"Not yet – it could have fallen over a very wide area of country."

"How's Serena taking it?"

"That's the weird thing, Geordie. On Tuesday their house was washed away during a storm. They haven't found her either. El Niño's been real active off the Pacific coast this year. Flash flooding up and down California. They say the creek turned into a raging torrent in minutes and roared through the valley, taking everything in its path. It's hard to imagine that sluggish old trickle being anything more than a glorified ditch."

'So — she's dead too?'

"That's the presumption, buddy. There was no warning so she didn't have the boat moored to the balcony. There was nothing left of the house, nothing at all. It was ripped off its foundations, smashed to rubble and swept downriver into the ocean. Apparently you'd never know there'd been a house there."

Geordie reflected on Matthew's comment that after he'd gone the Park system would bulldoze the site and plant willows. "Well, I guess that'll save the Park system the hassle of flattening the site."

"That's a bit harsh, man." Dan replied.

"Maybe, but somehow I think that's what Matthew wanted."

Chapter 7

Gabbot's Meadow

Geordie always headed west for the Labor Day weekend. It was a great time to take up unused vacation days while the weather was still fine, and use the opportunity to visit clients on the Coast afterwards. After an uneventful flight from Chicago he was met by his old pal, Chris Mason, in the Arrivals hall at San Francisco Airport.

Chris was a British friend who'd totally adopted the California outdoor and fitness ethos. He skied Tahoe every weekend in the winter, biked around San Francisco during the week, hiked the Sierras during summer, windsurfed around Alcatraz and jogged when he had nothing better to do. He was a rising banker at Wells Fargo but, as he'd put it succinctly over a campfire in the Sierras two years earlier, "I've reached the stage where my career is no longer important to me. I'm completely into lifestyle now." He was all of 28 at the time.

The more Presbyterian Geordie couldn't go quite that far, but admired Chris for his honesty. Not that Chris was unambitious — far from it. He just didn't see the point in busting his cojones for money when there were so many other interesting things to do.

That said, Geordie always enjoyed the distractions lined up by Chris whenever he came to town. The last time he was in the Bay Area Chris met him off the plane and announced, "I hope you're hungry because we're going straight to a carb party."

"A carb party?"

"We've got to carb up because tomorrow's the Bay-to-Breakers race."

"You're running in the Bay-to-Breakers?"

"So are you, mate. I've paid your entry fee and lined up your kit."

"But . . . I'm not even a runner," Geordie protested.

"Nor are 110,000 other people who enter for the race. There's a hard core of serious international marathon runners who line up at the start. They sprint away like gazelles when the pistol goes off and everyone else shambles along after them. The winners finish before most people have even passed the starting line."

"So it's not too arduous."

"Unless you call 50 lesbians bonded together to look like a Chinese dragon arduous, no."

So thanks to Chris Mason, Geordie had run the Bay-to-Breakers race the last time he was in San Francisco. He came in at number 16,789; Chris came in at 16,790, lagging one step behind to keep the pressure on Geordie. The only reason they didn't come in somewhere over 100,000 was that Chris had chartered a yacht in Oakland for the afternoon and they were in a hurry to get off and sail in the Bay.

Chris parked the Cherokee at the foot of a steep staircase that headed up a cliff towards Napier Street. "This is where you get out. If you carry your clobber up the steps, I'll park the car."

Geordie tramped up the steep steps with his tote bag, pausing for breath here and there until he reached a flower-bedecked alley called Napier Lane. A few years earlier Chris had purchased a wrecked shack on the cliff, surrounded by the rubble of an earthquake that happened in the 1950s. He worked furiously and turned it into a gorgeous property set in magnificent gardens, known widely to his friends as Popeye's Cabin. It had a splendid view of bohemian rooftops in the foreground and the Bay Bridge in the distance.

He brushed his way through the exotic foliage and met Angelina, Chris's lovely Guatemalan girlfriend, watering plants by the front door.

"Welcome to San Francisco."

Over a dinner of crisp vegetables, tuna and a glass of Sonoma Chardonnay, Chris discussed his plans for the week.

"Tomorrow we'll head up to the Sierras as usual. There's a range I'd like to explore called the Dardanelles. I thought we'd hike around there for three days, then finish the week by taking the raft down the Tuolomne River for a couple of days. On the way back we can take a side trip to Yosemite and hike up Half Dome." He saw the incredulity in Geordie's eyes, and added, "If there's time."

"Sounds wonderful. It's odd after all these years of hiking in the Sierras that we've never been to Yosemite."

"That's because it's a bit corny up there. Wall-to-wall mobile homes and campers crammed on the valley floor. A lot of shops and mass tourism, but it's worth exploring.'

"Everything's worth exploring," Geordie agreed.

After an early night in Popeye's Cabin they set out for the mountains at eight in the morning. They stopped at an outdoor shop in Oakland where Chris and Angelina bought a bag of camping widgets. Geordie was persuaded to purchase a mountaineer's backpack. "Crazy when you get back to Manhattan, but you won't regret it up in the Dardanelles," Chris commented.

They drove east for five hours across the dreary, parched Sacramento Valley until the road reached the magnificent pine forests of the Sierra foothills.

In mid-afternoon the Cherokee bumped into a rough car park. The silence was palpable when Chris turned off the engine. "This is as far into the Stanislaus National Forest as you're allowed to drive," he announced. Geordie stepped out of the vehicle and inhaled the warm air filled with the heady scent of pine resin.

"It's magnificent here." He stretched and yawned.

"Come on, get booted and spurred. We've got two miles before we reach our campsite at Rock Lake."

Geordie laced up his walking boots and heaved the new backpack over his shoulders. Angelina's pack was lighter than the boys' but she carried her share of food and common goods. They hiked along a trail through the darkening forest and pitched camp in a clearing by a lake as it was getting dark. As Chris padded around the campsite Geordie built a good fire while Angelina lined up filet mignons, onions, mushrooms, potatoes and peas. "This is the last fresh meal we get for a few days."

"Here – take a swig." Geordie passed a nondescript plastic bottle over the fire to Chris. He held it up to the firelight then sipped it cautiously. "Looks like a urine sample. What is it?"

"Bowmore, 18 years old. From Islay off the West Coast of Scotland."

"Can I try?" Geordie loved the way Angelina was game for anything. She sipped from the bottle and swilled the whisky thoughtfully around her mouth. Her eyes opened wide. After a few seconds she exclaimed, "Wow, that's intense!"

After the tents were pitched Chris fed a rope through the necks of the three rucksacks. "Hey give me a hand to carry these." They lugged the rucksacks a hundred yards away. Chris slung the rope over the highest branch of a gnarled pine. "OK – pull." They tugged and the rucksacks were lifted 30 feet aloft. Chris made the rope fast on a lower branch. "Right, that should be bear-proof for the night."

Geordie woke to the sound of splashing. He unzipped his tent flap. The early sunshine slanted through the pine branches as a light mist rose thinly off the water. Chris was a hundred yards out and waved from the centre of the lake. Angelina sat by the fire quietly, reviving the night's embers to heat up an Italian coffee percolator. Her black hair was loosely bundled into a bun. She wore a tee shirt and very little else. The three rucksacks still dangled in their tree like orange bags of cement. No bears last night.

"OK – can't let Mason get the better of me." He stripped off, ran to the shore, stood on a prominent rock, peered into the clear water to see how deep it was and plunged in. His head bobbed up again three seconds later. "Gordon . . . bloody . . . Bennett!" he gasped. "I thought this was supposed to be California."

"A bit brisk for you?" Chris turned his grinning face from a power crawl.

"Naa, it's fine." Geordie kicked slowly out to the centre of the lake, floated on his back to admire the scenery, and swam back.

An hour later they were dry, dressed and breakfasted. Everything in the camp was folded and packed into their backpacks, Chris spread out the embers from the fire, emptied his water bottle over anything that glowed, refilled it from the lake, popped in a water purification tablet and clipped it on his belt.

"Right, let's go."

They headed up a crumbling rocky trail. At first they were among heavy tree cover but as they gained altitude the vegetation thinned out. They hiked along a granite ridge with deep fissures, out of which grew tortuous and split pine stumps.

"These are Bristlecones." Angelina patted a convoluted branch. "The oldest living beings on the planet. This one might be 4000 years old."

"They look like dead Bonsai trees." Geordie peered for a sign of life among the branches. He found a few green shoots on the far side.

"Well, they are a bit like Bonsais if you think about it. The cone gets wedged in a crack in the rock, it germinates in the poorest soil you can imagine, gets practically no light, gets very little moisture and grows incredibly slowly. There is nowhere for the roots to go. This little twig over here could be 500 years old." Angelina tweaked a delicate shoot sticking out of a crevice.

In the early afternoon they reached a lush green meadow carpeted with lupines. A river tumbled down the rocks through the meadow. "Let's have a break for lunch." Chris didn't wait for a reply and dumped his backpack on the grass.

They stretched out in the sunshine. Chris studied the map, Angelina handed them bread, cheese and apples.

"I wonder how many people have ever been here?" Geordie mused.

"Very few, I'd say," Chris replied, studying the map. "Hang on. It's got a name. This place is called Gabbot's Meadow and that river's called Highland Creek."

"Who was Gabbot?"

"Oh probably a gold miner from the '49 Gold Rush days."

"Sounds plausible. I can see how a chap might have a few cows and horses grazing up here. It would be a good staging post as they explored further upcountry."

"I'm going to find a spot to cool off in the river," Angelina announced. She made her way down to the water and followed the river for 30 yards. Without self-consciousness she stripped off and waded into the water. She laughed and shouted back to the boys, "This is fe-ree-zing," then dived underwater completely. She re-emerged like a cork out of a bottle, flicked her hair back in a rainbow of droplets and splashed out of the water onto the shingle bank.

"You are one lucky fellow," Geordie said to Chris. "She's one of the most beautiful women I've ever seen."

"Yea, she's a good lady." Chris didn't seem to mind Geordie feasting his eyes on the body of his willowy girlfriend.

Angelina shouted, "This place is brilliant. I think we should stay here."

"We've still got three hours of hiking time today. If we stay we'll have to make up time tomorrow if we're going to get up the Dardanelles Dome," Chris replied.

"Oh come on, Honey, we're not on a business schedule. Why don't we just chill out here? We can pitch our tents and leave them with our backpacks, get up early tomorrow, hike to the Dome and get back here late afternoon. That way we won't have to tote our stuff along with us."

"Actually, that sounds like a good idea," Geordie weighed in. "We'll cover the extra miles much more easily if we're not carrying anything."

"Well, I'm cool if you're cool." Chris bowed to the consensus.

They set out their campsite on a flat promontory beside the river and built a fireplace with rocks from the bank. Geordie collected a stack of dry wood and made a pile of pine cones. The cones were six inches across and would make perfect fire-lighters. After taking what they needed out of their packs, they hauled them up a tall tree on the meadow's edge. They spent the rest of the afternoon loafing about, sunbathing and swimming, talking and fishing in a deep pool where the trout could be seen clearly at the bottom. They didn't catch any.

Chris and Angelina retired to their tent for an hour, which, while it filled Geordie with almost unbearable envy, gave him the opportunity to explore Gabbot's Meadow and take photographs in the lengthening shadows.

Outside the halo of flickering light that cocooned them around the campfire, the night was as black as could be imagined. It was a moonless sky, and they felt very small in the vastness of the universe among the unexplored mountains. Geordie lay awake for a long time after his companions had extinguished their lights and fallen silent. There was no wind. The only sound was the burbling water as it tumbled down the rocks past their tents.

He was settling into a hypnotic groove when the rhythm of the water seemed to change. Did something just interrupt the flow? It was surely his imagination. He drifted off. Again, the flow was interrupted. Something was in the water. "What the hell's that?" he said to himself. He felt his heart-rate increasing. He didn't want to wake the others or leave his tent for fear that he would attract the attention of whatever it was. A bear? A moose? A deer? A wolf? Or something altogether more sinister. An alien? Who was Gabbot? Was it a corruption of Gibbet? Did this lovely place harbour a ghastly secret?

An owl hooted very close to Geordie's tent. It was the sort of hoot that he'd heard in the movies when the French Resistance tried to call British agents after a parachute drop. Entirely fake, in other words. Were their tents about to be ransacked by a bunch of crazy mountain men? He reached for the Swiss army knife in the pocket of his tent, felt carefully for the notch of the biggest blade and pulled it out.

He was still holding the knife when Chris unzipped his tent flap at dawn and thrust a mug of coffee at him. "Come on, mate, time to get up. We've got six miles to hike to the base of the Dardanelles Dome this morning."

Geordie grunted, "Did you hear those noises last night around the camp?"

"No? What noises?"

"There was something in the water and an owl was hooting."

"Welcome to the Sierras. Remember, you're the stranger here, not the wildlife, mate."

Geordie heaved out of the sleeping bag and clambered down the bank to the river. He stripped and washed in the glacial water. The mist lay flat in the meadow and a small flock of sandpipers skittered away from him along the gravel shore.

After breakfast they secured the campsite and took a day-pack containing cameras, valuables and a picnic made by Angelina. By 7 a.m. they were on their way to the Dardanelles Dome. They followed Highland Creek through Gabbot's Meadow and into the trees. The mist was lifting slowly off the forest floor and the slant of the sun made the light in the valley look like a German Mystic painting.

"Do you think we'll see Bambi?" Angelina asked sweetly.

Four miles and 1200 feet later they reached an exquisite alpine meadow. Acres of marigolds, purple lupines, mountain willow and bromeliads were spread in front of them. They hiked through the meadow and climbed above the treeline to an altogether different plant zone. A wide soggy plain of heather, myrtle, bog cotton and lady's slipper stretched right up to the base of the Dome.

What looked like a picturesque mountain scene from afar became more daunting as they approached the rocks. Sinister vertical columns of black basalt towered above them. The cliffs soared 600 feet in places and offered no access.

"This reminds me of Fingal's Cave in the Hebrides," Geordie observed.

"What now, Captain?" Angelina was catching her breath. They were at 8000 feet and the going was tough.

"I don't want to force anyone to climb to the top of this thing," Chris panted, "but we've come all this way and I reckon we should try to find a way. I definitely think we should stick together, whatever we decide. What do you say?" Chris looked at his companions.

"It's still early in the day. We could follow the bottom of these columns for a while and see if there's a way up," Geordie suggested.

"Angelina?"

"I'm with you all the way."

They skirted the base for about a mile until they saw a chimney they could scramble up. The problem was that they had to traverse a steep snow field to reach the start of the steep gulley. It consisted of old snow, hardened into vertical ice waves by successive thawing and freezing. They were all wearing rubber-soled hiking boots with rounded toes. Chris stopped at the edge.

"These boots are great for trail hiking, but pretty lethal on ice. What do you think, folks?"

Geordie followed the ice field down with his eyes. The slope was about 70 degrees and tapered to a ragged end in a boulder–strewn rubble field a thousand feet below. "There's no stopping if we slip on this stuff."

"It's your call. I'll come back with you if we don't all agree. No recriminations."

"Let's do it." Angelina said quietly.

"OK, here's what I suggest," Chris began. "There won't be much traction on this stuff. Imagine you're skiing. Don't lean into the mountain, but try to keep as vertical as possible. That way you put your weight more squarely on the ice rather than at an angle. It'll give you the best chance." He looked at Angelina and Geordie. "Sure? Once we start we'll have to keep going forward."

"Yup. Let's do it." Geordie said firmly. In truth he hated heights. He hadn't experienced anything like this on any previous hike in the Sierras.

Angelina pursed her lips and nodded.

Chris led the way by kicking a first step into the ice. It was fairly soft. It was late morning and the sun had begun its daily thawing process.

"This is easier than I thought," Chris said as he made solid progress across the ice field.

Angelina and Geordie followed a few yards behind. Geordie kept his focus firmly on Chris's footsteps. He was too nervous to look up at the looming black basalt towers or down at the boulders far below. Chris continued with a steady rhythm and Geordie began to feel confident that they were home and dry. Chris halted. They'd reached a patch of snow in the shadow of the cliffs.

"This is pure bloody ice. I can't kick a foothold in it."

Geordie looked down for the first time. The view was like being at the top of a gigantic Olympic ski jump. Blue sheet ice stretched all the way down to the rock field a long, long way below. They had about 60 yards to go. He suddenly became weary and his legs turned rubbery with fear.

"So, what do you suggest?"

"We have to keep going — remember to walk vertically and keep your weight pressing downwards, not at an angle. Try to move as fast as possible. If you slip, your momentum will take you forwards. You'll end up slipping at an angle and you'll move towards the edge of the ice field rather than falling all the way to the bottom."

"Come on guys. The more we think about it the worse it'll get. Just go forward, Chris." Geordie steeled himself.

Chris started by moving forward at a fast pace. He slipped, slid downhill a few feet and stopped. After repeating this manoeuvre he reached the far side about 80 feet below from where he started. Angelina and Geordie arrived at more or less the same spot. They collapsed on the heather as soon as they'd made the crossing.

"I don't mind admitting I was shit-scared," Geordie said, looking downhill. "We could have been smashed on those rocks far below."

"No guts, no glory." Chris swigged from his water bottle. "Come on mate, onwards and upwards." He patted Geordie on the shoulder.

The chimney was indented and eroded and they grabbed tufts of vegetation to help themselves up. As they were climbing, Angelina shouted, "Hey, look at that." She pointed at a large rock carving on the cliff face well away from the chimney. "How did anyone manage to do that?"

It portrayed a figure with its arms out to the side, trailing feathers under the arms. Its legs and body were human, but the face was pointed like a bird's. It was at least 10 feet tall and 8 wide. It reminded Geordie of a crude version of an Egyptian wall-carving.

The chimney led up to the rim of the cliff, where, with one final heave, they lay panting on the edge of the basalt pillars. They were at nearly 9000 feet.

"So, Chris, what did you make of that rock carving?"

"Haven't a clue. I'll check the guidebook when we get back to camp."

"It must have had a religious significance for them to risk swinging out over those cliffs to carve it."

"I wonder if it's aligned with any features in the mountains?" Angelina stood on the cliff directly above the carving. "There's a notch in a mountain over there, but there's no logical link."

"Maybe they just hurled their prisoners over the edge. Like our medieval witch trials — if they flew they were innocent. If they crashed onto the rocks they were guilty," Geordie joked.

The sun was high as they trudged the final 200 feet to the top of the Dome. The air was filled with a sickly stench and they were plagued by thousands of flies.

"Something died around here." Geordie gagged. It was made worse by the altitude as they gasped deeply for air.

They stood to get their breath back while admiring the 40 mile view of the Stanislaus National Forest and beyond. A brass surveyors' button was hammered crudely into a rock to mark the summit.

"Let's get out of here. It smells real bad." Angelina blocked her face with a kerchief.

The eight-mile hike back to the campsite was a long trudge, but downhill and they were travelling light. After climbing the Dardanelles Dome in a 15-mile loop, it was a welcome sight to see Gabbot's Meadow bathed in the late afternoon sunshine, and their tents pitched by the river.

"I'm knackered." Geordie collapsed onto a mossy patch by his tent. "We've been hiking solidly for 10 hours."

"Who wants some tea?" A wisp of smoke rose as Angelina lit a small pile of pinecones.

"I smell like a polecat. I'm going to wash." Chris threw off his clothes and dived into the Highland Creek. "Holy shit!" he gasped, scrubbing the dirt and sweat off himself vigorously in the water. "I bet this is meltwater off that ice field we crossed this morning."

They cleaned up and relaxed as the sun sank over the Western ranges. The Bowmore was passed around the fire and they munched on peanuts. Chops sizzled in the pan. In the firelight Chris paraphrased from his guide to the Sierras.

"The Indians in this area are thought to been the Paiutes. There was a tribe around Yosemite called the Mi-Wuks, but I'll settle for the Paiutes. They were pretty much wiped out by white settlers a hundred years ago. They were known for their petroglyphs — rock carvings. The petroglyphs were carved by shamans and were made in places where they believed special energy came from the rock face. A carving of concentric circles would highlight a spot which the shaman believed radiated particularly strong energy."

"That's like some theories about standing stones and ley lines in ancient Britain," Geordie said, "We've got some pretty serious energy lines around us in Balnadarg in Scotland."

Other themes in the Paiute petroglyphs included horses, arrows, birds and the Bird Man, which had a particular religious significance to them.

Chris flicked through the chapter. "It doesn't say what the religious significance was."

"Do you think that was a Bird Man we saw carved up on the Dome?" Angelina asked.

"Bingo!" Chris said. "Here are some photos of Paiute carvings." He passed the book around.

"Hey, there's the Bird Man!" Angelina exclaimed. "His arms are stretched out with feathers underneath, his legs are spread and his face has a beak. Just like the guy we saw today. It says here that shamans controlled the magic of the tribe. The peak of magic was the ability to metamorphose into animals, particularly birds, which were the apex of spirituality. To be a Bird Man was therefore the highest aspiration among the Paiutes."

"How was it carved 500 feet up on a cliff?" Chris asked.

"It wasn't far from the top. They must have lowered a guy on a rope to do the carving," replied Angelina.

So they talked on about shamans, religious healers, herbalists and ley lines. Geordie shared his recent experience of animism in Africa, Chris spoke of mysterious lines he'd seen in the Andes, Angelina described lost pyramids in the Guatemalan jungle.

They were stretched out by the fire after a very satisfying meal. As on the previous night it was pitch black but for the twinkling of distant stars. There was no wind and the only sound in the wilderness was the water flowing in the creek running by their tents.

"Did you hear that?" Geordie interrupted their contented murmurings.

"Hear what?" Chris asked with a laugh, flinging another log on the fire in a shower of sparks.

"That," Geordie repeated.

Angelina sat up, looking alarmed. "I can hear a drumming noise. It's getting louder."

A rolling sound was coming at them through the meadow. "Bloody hell, it sounds like a herd of buffalo coming at us down the hill!" Geordie shouted.

"There aren't any buffaloes in this part of the United States." Chris sounded calm but was nevertheless alarmed.

"Not in this dimension," Geordie said, harking back to their recent conversation.

Two horses materialized out of the darkness. They had a wild look in the eye as they galloped full tilt towards them. "They're coming straight at us. They're crazy!" Angelina screamed.

The three friends braced to meet a collision when suddenly the horses veered away and thundered off, left and right, into the blackness of Gabbot's Meadow. Before they vanished, one of them slowed, cocked its tail and dumped on the grass on the edge of their campsite. A Paiute Bird Man was branded on the horse's haunch.

Chapter 8

The Great Experiment

In January 1991 Geordie Kinloch was one of millions of Americans who slowed their pace on their way to work to watch TV monitors in malls, office buildings, railroad stations, coffee shops and hotel lobbies. President Bush was coordinating a powerful Coalition to add muscle to the UN Resolution that Saddam Hussein should withdraw from Kuwait. But there was serious apprehension in the USA. What about the Republican Guards? How will we deal with the casualties of Weapons of Mass Destruction? The last time we had the French as allies. . . .

Geordie had just entered his office from a skin-stripping wind-chill of 68 degrees below zero when the phone rang.

"Hi there, it's Jay. Got a few minutes?"

"Sure. What's up?" Jayanthkumar V Panday was one of his oldest friends in Chicago. He was in a crowd of young Indian doctors who had come to study in the early 1980s, stayed to work in the city and prospered mightily. Geordie originally met him at the West Bank Sports Club, where they were well matched in squash and tennis.

"You know I've been in America now for eight years? Well, I've held my Green Card for five and I'm told that I can now apply for US citizenship."

Six months earlier Jay had taken up a professorship at a famed medical school in Wisconsin. His friends Rajiv and Sami were also professors. Rajiv was a professor of electro cardiology in Iowa and Sami ran a viral research team at a university in downstate Illinois.

"Really?" Geordie switched his friend to the speakerphone while he peeled off his thermal layers.

"Yes. And so could you, I'm sure."

"Why would I want to become a US citizen? My green card gives me all the rights I need in this country. Besides, nothing wrong with being British, is there?"

"No. But if you have the opportunity to be a citizen of the USA, you should take it. You don't need to give up your British citizenship. You then have the right to work in the two great economic zones of the world – the USA and the European Union."

"Sounds fancy."

"Well, of course in my case it would mean that I could work in America, the European Union and India."

"If all you want is to work here, why complicate your life by becoming an American, particularly if you ever want to work back home or in Europe at some point? You're already allowed to work here and you're a famous professor."

"Because it is a *privilege* to be offered American citizenship, Geordie."

"If you say so." Geordie had to laugh. When Jay said privilege he rolled the 'r' and sounded like a British comedian mimicking an Indian-English accent.

"So I take it you wouldn't be interested in becoming an American with us?"

"Us?"

"Rajiv and Sami are considering taking this step too."

"Well I'm sure America will be proud to have you all. You'll be a huge asset to the nation."

"I still need your help, Geordie."

'Of course. How?'

'Well, you're a lawyery kind of guy, and it would be very kind if you could take us through the paperwork. If we met for a drink, could you look through the forms with me and see if they're OK before we submit them?'

"I'm not an immigration lawyer, or any other kind of lawyer, you know, but I'd be happy to help you through your paperwork if you like."

"Thank you very much. I'll give you brain surgery any time you want it."

"Sounds like a fair deal. When d'you want to get together?"

They met at the West Bank Club the following day after work. Jayanthkhumar brought three blank Applications to File — Petitions for Naturalization. One for himself and one each for Rajiv and Sami.

"These are just play sheets. I thought we could run through the questions and make a mess of these forms. Once we've got the right answers I'll take them home and we'll each fill out fresh forms for submission."

"Sounds like a good plan. Let's go." For a Brit like Geordie the questions seemed ludicrously simple. It was clear what the Immigration Service was fishing for and easy to avoid the pitfalls. Jay wasn't so clearly in tune with the American neurosis.

"Question 3. Are you now, or have you ever, in the United States or in any other place, been a member of, or in any other way connected or associated with the Communist Party? Yes or No?"

"When I was a student in Lahore I wrote for the university Communist Party newspaper. We were all Communists then," Jay replied enthusiastically.

"So that's a No, then." Geordie ticked the box on the form.

"No, Geordie, it's a Yes," Jay exclaimed. "I'm very proud to be Communist."

"I don't think Uncle Sam would be too thrilled to let a Communist into the country, even if he is a top professor of medicine. Americans detest communism to the last drop of their blood. They died fighting it in Korea, in Vietnam, and I dare say may one day die fighting it in Russia or China."

"I will not deny my communist beliefs."

"Jay, you're no more communist than my Aunt Fanny. You drive a Mercedes, you wear tailor-made suits, you earn a fortune as a professor of surgery. And here we are eating dinner in that hotbed of communism, the West Bank Club in Chicago. Believe me, Jay, you and your fellow doctors need to embrace capitalism for this gig."

"All right, all right. Tick the No box." Jay was crestfallen.

"I already did. Question 4, next page. Do you believe in the Constitution and form of government of the United States?"

"They really have no right to ask these questions. They really are very personal."

"Well?"

"Oh all right, Yes." Jay was getting steamed up.

"Good lad. Question 6: If the law requires it, are you willing to bear arms on behalf of the United States?"

"Most certainly not. I come here to work, not to fight."

"It's a fairly safe bet, I'd say. You're older than the draft age."

"In that case, Yes."

So they completed the Petition for Naturalization. Geordie sorted through the remaining pile of immigration papers.

"You need to submit fingerprints with your application. Take a look – there are specific instructions for applicants for citizenship." Geordie slid a sheet across the table to Jay. It was entitled Federal Bureau of Investigation United States Department of Justice Washington DC 20537 APPLICANT.

Jay scanned the paper. "Bloody hell! How do I go about finding a law enforcement agent who will do my fingerprints?"

"Easy. There's a guy in the basement of a building on South LaSalle who'll do it. I'll get the address. You just show up and take your place in the queue."

"OK. Is that all?" Jay didn't enquire how Geordie knew so much about getting fingerprinted in Chicago.

"No sir. After you send these forms and the fingerprints to the Immigration Department you will need to apply for an interview. Before they let you take the Pledge of Allegiance they want to know that you're knowledgeable enough to become an American. Here's a booklet prepared by a law firm to assist you in preparing for passing the citizenship requirements under the Immigration and Nationality Act." Geordie passed the booklet over to Jay, who was exasperated.

"Do you mean — I have to learn the answers to these 100 questions?"

"They're not that complicated. Here, let me test you." Geordie snatched the booklet from Jay and opened it at random. "Right — what is the capital of Illinois?"

"Springfield."

"Who said 'Give me liberty or give me death'?"

"That's easy." Jay beamed, "Karl Marx."

"You're joking."

"Absolutely not. It was a rallying call on the street for the proletariat Bolsheviks as they were overthrowing the old regime in Russia."

"You and your bloody communism. They don't want to hear that here, OK? The answer is Patrick Henry."

"Who's Patrick Henry?"

"I haven't the faintest idea but do NOT refer to communism, Russia or any of that left-wing stuff during your interview. Anything that sounds remotely revolutionary and heroic in this questionnaire must have been said by an American. Just say Thomas Jefferson if you don't know an answer. OK? At least you'll get points for trying. How many branches are there in our government?"

"I don't know, Geordie." Jay replied.

"Three. The Legislative, the Executive and the Judiciary. What is the date of Independence Day?"

"I know that. July 4th."

"Very good. Independence from whom?"
"France?"
"You're joking, I hope."
"England, then."
"OK. What are the colours of our flag?"
"Red, white and blue."
"Very good — not that complicated, is it? I suggest you take this booklet and learn it by heart. They won't ask questions outside this booklet, I'm sure." Geordie picked out another random question: "One more. Name three rights or freedoms guaranteed by the Bill of Rights."
"What's the Bill of Rights?"
"Jay, you've got to know this stuff. Becoming an American is not a trivial thing that you do on your afternoon off in Chicago. People die to become US citizens. People die to protect the rights of Americans. You have to show respect for this country and the process of naturalization." Geordie surprised himself with the earnestness of his lecture.
"If you say so," Jay replied, adding, "I really must get back to Wisconsin tonight. I have a very early start in the hospital tomorrow morning."
Miraculously Jay and his friends buckled down to learn the answers set out in the booklet. On the morning of Jay's interview with his immigration officer, Geordie woke him with a call: "Who has the power to declare war?"
"The Congress."
"Very good. Who was President during the Civil War?"
"Abraham Lincoln."
"Good. It looks like you've done some work on this project. How are you feeling about the whole thing?"
"I feel fine, but it's such a waste of time. They should be fast-tracking me and let me keep on my critical path as a surgeon in the

hospital, rather than asking me questions about events that took place 200 years ago."

"You gotta play the game, my friend. The point of this process is that everyone who becomes a citizen has got at least some common ground with his compatriots."

"I've got to get to Chicago. I'll talk to you later." Jay hung up.

At four o'clock the same afternoon Jay called Geordie from his Mercedes. He was heading up the Edens Expressway on his return to Madison.

"How did it go?"

"The guy was Chinese. I could hardly understand his English. The interview ended rather abruptly. He asked me a question about the Vice President. I said, 'Do you mean our current Vice President?' He got irritated and said something like, 'No, Vice Plesident loll in Hou of Leplesentative.' I said, 'That must be Dan Quayle.' He marked his sheet of paper, sighed and said, 'That all light. You go now.' So I left the interview."

The spectacle of an Indian mimicking a Chinese speaking English in an interview to become American appealed to Geordie. "Was he angry?"

"I don't think so."

"I mean, did he cut short the interview because he thought you were taking the piss out of him, or did it run its course?"

"It went all right up to that point. He ticked a lot of boxes as we spoke."

Jay, Rajiv and Sami succeeded in jumping through the bureaucratic hoops and were duly invited to Immigration Hearings at the McKinley Dirksen building on February 14th, a rich date in Chicago's collective memory.

Jay invited Geordie to attend the event as a friend and witness. Several hundred people filed into the courtroom. There were no

Caucasians being inducted that day. Geordie counted Vietnamese, Chinese, Hispanics, Somalis, West Africans, Arabs, Jews, Syrians and, of course, his little knot of Indians. It was a true mishmash of humanity, everyone applying for American citizenship on their own agenda. But they had all taken the oath of allegiance and were deemed suitable to become Americans, so here they were to take the final step.

A large woman in a tight blue uniform stepped up to the podium and announced in a shrill voice,

"Will everyone please rise for the entry of the judge."

A white man in robes entered. "Please be seated."

Jay was getting restive. He leaned over to his friends and said in a stage whisper, "I really wish this bloody thing would hurry up. I've got to get back to Madison." Sami looked at his Rolex, replying, "My car's parked on Wacker and it costs me $10 for every hour or part of an hour." Rajiv sat with his arms crossed, a thunderous expression on his face.

The judge took his seat. The woman in uniform addressed the crowd again, "Please would you open the booklet on Page 2. We will all now say together the American's Creed." She led the crowd,

"I believe in the United States of America as a Government of the People, by the People, for the People, whose just powers are derived from the consent of the governed; a democracy in a republic; a sovereign nation . . . '

Rajiv looked at his watch impatiently. He shook his head. Sami whispered something to him. Jay looked at the ceiling. None of them made an attempt to mime the words, let alone speak them. They all had the same expression: This is quite absurd. What a complete waste of important peoples' time. Geordie was rather enjoying the occasion and chimed in loudly for the last sentence of the Creed: "I therefore believe it is my duty to my country to love it, to support its

Constitution, to obey its laws, to respect its flag, and to defend it against all enemies."

They were invited to take their seats again. The judge seemed a kindly man. He walked to the podium and began: "Welcome to this auspicious day. I want everyone in this courtroom to turn to the person on their left and to the person on their right, in front and behind them. I want you all to shake hands. Today you have become citizens of the United States of America. You are part of a great experiment. It is an experiment which has a long way to play out. What you do with your lives as Americans and how you hold yourselves in the world will have a major impact on the future of this country and the lives of your grandchildren . . ."

Geordie loved the sense of inclusion that was being conferred on the new citizens, and was annoyed with Jay for treating the occasion as an inconvenience. He appeared increasingly exasperated and kept looking at his watch, whispering with his friends. Geordie put a finger to his lips as a signal to be quiet – or at least respectful – but Jay ignored it.

At the end of his 10-minute homily the judge walked to one end of the platform and stood under an American flag. "Now, ladies and gentlemen, we will pledge allegiance to the Flag."

"For goodness sake, this is such hocus pocus. I really need to get back to Champaign," said Sami. Fortunately, none of his immediate neighbours appeared to understand English – or at least were too polite to acknowledge the insult to their newly adopted citizenship.

The judge stood erect with his right hand over his heart, leading the crowd in saying the Pledge: "I pledge allegiance to the flag of the United States of America and to the Republic for which it stands, one Nation under God, indivisible, with liberty and justice for all."

Geordie was warmed to behold African, Vietnamese, Mexican and Chinese men and women of all ages struggling to be word perfect, hands on hearts with tears streaming down their faces. Clearly, becoming American was the culmination of a very long road for some of them.

The judge wrapped up: "Congratulations to all of you and welcome to the God-given unalienable rights which the Constitution of the United States bestows on you as the natural right of all men."

People of all the ethnic backgrounds smiled and hugged, clapped and shook hands. Jay slapped Sami's back. Rajiv commented sourly, "That's great. Now let's go."

The large lady with the tight blue uniform returned to the podium. "Would everybody please stand as the judge leaves the courtroom. When he leaves you are at liberty to sit down again. Please stay in your seats for a few moments as we have an important announcement to make." She left.

Rajiv was close to the end of his tether. "For goodness sake. I've got a flight to catch to Des Moines and important work to get on with."

Geordie tried to chivvy him up. "Don't worry. It's just a few more minutes. Enjoy the experience."

The large lady returned to the podium, accompanied by two heavily armed policemen, Chicago's finest. She tapped on the microphone. She read from a sheet of paper: "Would the following new American citizens please make themselves known to myself or my two colleagues here. Would Doctors Jayanthkumar Panday, Rajiv Patel and Sami Muckerjee please come to the front of the room."

Jay froze. Rajiv and Sami looked dumbstruck. Geordie wondered what was going on. Perhaps someone had fainted and this was a variation on "Is there a doctor in the house?" The crowd instinctively parted around the three of them. "We're here," Jay shouted. "What do you want?"

The two cops made their way up an aisle towards the group. "Dr Panday? Dr Muckerjee, Dr Patel?" one of them enquired politely.

"Yes, that's us. We're just heading back to our universities."

"You are required to report to The Great Lakes Naval Station at 0900 hours tomorrow for training."

"Training?" Jay gaped at the policeman.

"Yes sir. Your services are required by the US armed forces."

Rajiv's dander rose. "You can't do this. We're civilian professors of medicine. I have an important engagement this evening in Des Moines."

Geordie was astounded, asking, "My friends need more time. They need to arrange their affairs. They can't just abandon their lives. Is there a right of appeal?"

"Your friends can discuss these questions in front of the Selection Board tomorrow." The cop replied.

"Selection Board? Oh, so that means they haven't been drafted?"

"Not yet, sir, but by applying for US citizenship they agreed to bear arms on behalf of the United States, if the law requires it. Also they agreed to perform non-combatant services in the Armed Forces of the United States, if the law requires it. They took the Pledge of Allegiance, sir. I understand there is an urgent requirement for qualified medical personnel in the Gulf. Your friends can discuss their options in front of the Selection Board tomorrow."

Rajiv leaned forward in his chair with his head in his hands. Sami and Jay stood gaping at the cop. Geordie understood in a flash what was meant by the phrase, 'Time froze'. The three of them might have turned to pillars of salt at Gomorrah.

Geordie was rather pleased that he hadn't taken up the offer to become an American citizen. He patted an appalled Jay on the back. "Just remember, when you come out of the army you'll have the right to work in two great economic zones of the world."

Jay finally saw the humour of his situation "And India, Geordie. Don't forget India."

Chapter 9

Moving from New York

The twin-funnelled tugboat ripped through the ice floes as it towed a cavernous rusted steel barge up the Hudson River. Plumes of steam curled from the top of skyscrapers, crystallizing in the wind-chill. The early-morning January sunshine set a million panes of glass on fire as Manhattan busied itself for another day.

Geordie stood at the window of his warm apartment with a mug of tea cradled in his hands. He watched the muffled figures far below, scurrying left and right, east and west. From this vantage they were meaningless ciphers criss-crossing a vast concrete apron, mere insects. He was euphoric. After a long stint as one of those very insects, Geordie was now leaving New York City for good.

He slotted a CD into the machine and, with a primal 'Yee-Haa', slipped into the shower to the crazy chords of Duane Allman's guitar. Ten minutes later he emerged, towelled his pinkish body, and slumped, dishevelled, into a reclining chair. Geordie found a name at random in the Business Pages and picked up the phone.

"Good morning. I'm calling to arrange for the contents of my apartment to be shipped back to the UK."

"Can you indicate the size of the apartment and volume of contents?" a bored female voice replied. Geordie imagined the woman filing her nails as she spoke.

"It's a small place, one bedroom."

"Square feet?"

"About 900."

"OK – how much furniture?"

"A bed, a sofa, two armchairs, a small table, six paintings, some rugs, lamps, odds and ends . . ."

"OK – what value?"

"I don't know – 100K, maybe?" Geordie was humiliated to admit to a total stranger how little the contents of his paltry apartment were worth. He hated himself even more for exaggerating the value of his stuff by a factor of four, if he was being honest about it.

"OK – I get the picture. Look, buddy, here at InterGlobal Freightways we ship by the container-load. You need to speak to a Load Consolidator. They specialize in part loads and they'll tell ya real fast how much space in a container your furniture needs to take up. They'll then find you a container heading 'cross the Atlantic and charge you for the cubic metres that your stuff takes up. OK?"

"Can you recommend a Load Consolidator?"

"Sure – not a recommendation but you can call Zipfreight in Queens."

"Zipfreight in Queens?"

"Yea. Tell them I sent you. Goodbye."

Geordie hung up and called Zipfreight.

"This is Cliff, can I help you?"

Geordie went through the same spiel he'd just delivered to the woman at InterGlobal Freightways, adding, "I understand that you ship smaller amounts from New York to the UK."

"Sure. What's your email? We only deal by email at Zipfreight. That way we always get an audit trail and nobody gets upset."

"Fair enough." That sounded faintly ominous but Geordie gave his email address.

Five minutes later he received a questionnaire. Among other things it requested a list of items to be shipped from New York to the UK, their approximate value, the date of pick-up and the preferred mode of transport (Air Freight or Ocean Transport). It was padded with enough official verbiage to give Geordie reason to believe he was in efficient hands.

Customer is subject to custom clear their goods upon arrival and responsible for any port charges, duties and/or taxes if applicable at destination and then responsible to pick up their shipment from the designated warehouse. For a negotiated charge we will arrange a full service to cover all these items.

Note: should you require insurance coverage for the full value of your shipment please contact our insurance broker at Carter International prior to your scheduled move to set up an All Risk Insurance Certificate to cover your shipment for its full value.

With rockabilly music blaring from the radio, Geordie pottered around his apartment flourishing a yellow legal pad and a pencil. He made a list of every item for Zipfreight, so they could estimate the cost of shipping his stuff across the Atlantic. He itemized larger items like chairs, tables, the bed and sofa. He categorized his smaller effects into boxes (breakables) and boxes (non-breakables). He then sat at his laptop, typed the list and sent it by email to Zipfreight in Queens.

Minutes later Cliff responded.

On the basis of the information you gave us, the cost of transportation will be $8000. That includes approximately $300 for wooden crating of your paintings, $700 for packing; $325 per cubic meter for Atlantic freight and $1000 for pick up and delivery. Estimated 400 cubic feet after it's all been boxed.

Is that door to door, all expenses paid?

Yes sir. Door to door, all expenses paid.

That sounds fine. Can you pick up on Thursday 22nd?

Sure. What about insurance?

Add it to the bill.

You need to call Carter International directly. It's a conflict of interest for me to set up your insurance.

Geordie called Carter International, based in Shreveport, Louisiana. He emailed Carter International the same inventory he'd just sent to Cliff. In a few minutes they responded.

We are prepared to offer you the concessionary premium offered to favored customers of Zipfreight. Insurance for shipping and transporting your furniture and effects from a point in New York City to a point in Scotland will be $2300.

Twenty pages of finely drafted Terms and Conditions were attached to the email. He called Carter International.

"That's a bit steep."

'It's our price for accepting your risk. If your container gets lost or impaired through accident, shipwreck, acts of God, terrorism or other causes as set out in Appendix iv, we will reimburse you. If you accept this insurance all the risk falls on the insurance company; if you don't accept this insurance, all the risk falls on you."

'Mm – fair enough."

"We will activate insurance cover on receipt of a banker's draft in our favor." They gave details of a PO Box address in Shreveport where the draft should be express mailed. Steep, but it all seemed in order to Geordie.

He pulled on his grey donkey jacket, scarf, gloves and an Elmer Fudd-style hat with ear flaps. Nodding at Templeton, the Jamaican concierge behind his apartment's reception desk, he ventured into the bitter cold. He pulled the scarf across his mouth in the stinging air and headed towards the preposterously named World Financial Center. His bank drew up a draft in favour of Carter International and Geordie sent it to Shreveport by Express Delivery.

In the 10 days before his effects were due to be picked up, Geordie indulged in an orgy of retail therapy in New York. He bought a reclining leather armchair destined for his study at Balnadarg, sheets, crockery, CDs, clothes and all manner of electronic gadgets for a small fraction of their cost in the UK. It was all delivered to his apartment, where he spent hours removing labels, packaging and other signs of recent purchase to minimize the chance of unusual attention from UK customs officers.

He arranged with the building's management to reserve the freight elevator for the morning of the move. He paid the $100 reservation fee and everything was in order.

At 8 o'clock on the appointed morning his internal phone rang. It was Templeton in the lobby. "Mr Kinloch, sir, the movers are here."

"Send them up."

A man in a sleeveless shirt came to the door. "My name is Herman Velasquez. I will be organizing your move today." Herman was a slender, short, wiry man with slicked black hair. He looked uncannily like Freddy Mercury. "Perhaps you could show me the furniture we will be taking."

"Everything you see in the apartment goes, except that suitcase in the corner."

Herman nodded at the men who had come up behind him.

Two other fellows entered the apartment. Like a black interpretation of Laurel & Hardy, one was round and tall, the other short and skinny. "This is Cassius and Muhamed, Mr Kinloch."

The men started by dismantling the bed and packed its component parts into boxes which were numbered and marked 'BED' with black indelible ink. And so on, with 'CHAIR', 'CLOTHES', 'KITCHEN' and all the rest of Geordie's stuff. Everything was systematically packed, labelled and carted carefully along the corridor to the freight elevator. It was like one of those time-lapse films of a body being demolished on the Serengeti. The first shot was of a newly killed zebra – his apartment at 8 a.m. that morning. The second showed lionesses tearing off limbs – his bed, bulky furniture, Persian rugs. The third was of secondary predators, hyenas and vultures, up to their necks in gore as they tugged on intestines and sinews – his CDs and Savile Row suits. The final shot was of a bleached pile of bones lying inert on the savannah – his apartment at 10.15 that morning.

The entire contents of his life in New York were packed and removed in two hours. Herman Velasquez kept tabs and prepared an elaborate inventory as they worked. As the last dolly trundled down the corridor he signed the last page, got Geordie to countersign, tore off a pink customer copy, took a money order for $8000 and vanished down the freight elevator.

Geordie filled his one remaining mug with coffee and walked across the echoing apartment to the balcony. Far below he saw an unmarked white van speeding out of the street, turning left at the light and heading north towards Mid Town Manhattan. He had two hours to shower, dress, pack his personal effects and take a cab to Newark.

Geordie settled back into the eternal cycle of life at Balnadarg. Late January in Scotland was milder, if gloomier, than New York. Snowdrops carpeted the woods, daffodils were showing green shoots through the forest floor. Sleet scored across the fields, but didn't lie for long. In a few weeks the heifers would calve and the ewes (yows, they called them) start to drop their lambs. The contrast between New York City and Balnadarg lifestyles was extreme. Geordie found himself paying unusual attention to the Highland folk. Listening to their straight, uncomplicated talk was music compared to the universal duplicity which masqueraded as street smarts in New York.

"It's March 20th, Honey. Shouldn't your shipment be arriving from America by now?" his wife Josie asked one evening over dinner.

"I suppose it should. I haven't really focused on it. They reckoned it would take about six weeks to ship across the Atlantic. We're now at, let me see . . . " Geordie closed his eyes and calculated back to mid-January. "Goodness, they've had eight weeks. I'll email them in the morning."

The response from Zipfreight in New York the following day was dense, but informative.

> Port of Departure Buenos Aires. Port of Destination Antwerp. Bill of Lading 4746011. Trailer 1803, Geordie Kinloch. Items: 16 crates. Household Goods and personal effects. Gross weight 2123 lbs. Measurement 18.492 cu M.
>
> Please be advised that cargo was delivered to Maldon Essex on March 7th. Incurring demurrage at a rate of £12.50 per day for the first 7 days, £17 per day thereafter. You should liaise with Ms Laredo Buzzard in England at the following number . . .

"Bloody hell. They've had it in the country since March 7th. They might have let me know.' Another swift calculation came up with the sum of £200 in demurrage charges. He called the gloriously named Ms Laredo Buzzard.

"Good morning – Zipfreight International."

"May I speak to Ms Laredo Buzzard, please."

"Speaking." Geordie had expected a Texas drawl but he got Thames Estuary.

"Yes, I was given your name by your colleague Cliff, in New York. You're holding some cargo for me. My name is Geordie Kinloch."

"Cliff? Are we now? Do you have a Bill of Lading number?"

"Yes. It's 4746011."

"I need to see the original Bill of Lading documents. Can you send them to me please?"

"I don't have any original documentation. It was all dealt with by Cliff in New York."

"Cliff?" Laredo Buzzard sounded dubious.

"Yes. Cliff. In New York. He's your man there," Geordie said sarcastically. He felt impatience boiling up in him.

"I don't think so, darlin'. I speak to New York every day. There's no Cliff in our office over there."

"Fair enough then, are you holding my shipment or not?"

"Let me check against your Bill of Lading number. Give me a minute."

Geordie heard Laredo Buzzard tapping furiously on a keyboard.

"It looks like we have a shipment. It's been on demurrage since March 7th. Have you made arrangements for longer-term storage?"

"No." Geordie was exasperated. "I only became aware of you holding my shipment yesterday and I'm trying to track it down. What do I need to do to get it from you to me?"

"You'll need a Customs Clearance Declaration form. Customs will need to see your Bill of Lading. You'll then need to discharge your demurrage costs and arrange to have your crates shipped from Essex to Scotland."

"I see. How long will all of that take?"

"Depends how soon you get the Bill of Lading to us."

"And I pay demurrage all the while?"

"Yes, sir."

"Can't you stop the clock on that while the paperwork is done?"

"No, sir. Storage is expensive."

Geordie ferreted desperately through his papers to find a Bill of Lading. He was certain he had never had one, and that it had all been dealt with by Zipfreight in New York. He emailed Cliff:

Hate to tell you this, but they've never heard of you at Zipfreight in the UK. Can you forward a Bill of Lading to them ASAP so that I can get my stuff out of storage?

Shortly afterwards Laredo Buzzard called him. "We've received a

Bill of Lading from the forwarders in New York. Now what we need is a banker's draft for £2768.67 to arrange customs clearance and shipping to your address in Scotland."

"I thought I had already paid for shipping everything from door to door."

"Not according to our records. It's only paid as far as port of arrival."

"Leave it with me." Geordie emailed Cliff again.

What's going on here, Cliff? I now have to pay over $5000 to clear customs. I thought you had covered all costs from my apartment in New York City to my house in Scotland. Please clarify.

Dead bollock silence.

A day later he called Laredo Buzzard, "Your guy in New York has some dubious business practices. Anyway, I need to get this sorted out. I'll send a draft for the amount you need. Then I'd appreciate if you'd get everything shipped to my house."

Josie wasn't happy.

"This doesn't feel right,'" she shook her head. "The cost of shipping contents from a small New York apartment is going to cost as much as what you're shipping. You paid $7000 for shipping, $2300 for insurance, hundreds of pounds for demurrage – whatever that is – now £2768 for customs clearance. For what? $50,000 worth of stuff, max?"

"Don't worry about it," Geordie said airily, although he felt far from airy. "Once we get the stuff here we'll forget the pain."

"Something doesn't feel right. I think you should contact the police before you send your customs clearance draft to them."

"The police? That's a bit far-fetched. Look, we're not in the habit of getting our stuff shipped around the world. This is an unusual experience for us. It feels strange, but only because we're trying to understand a complex transaction that's new to us. Demurrage and customs charges go on all the time. The point of demurrage is to encourage people to shift their stuff from the dockside as quickly as possible. Keeps trade moving."

"Not convinced, Honey." Josie replied worriedly as she looked up from her computer.

Laredo Buzzard faxed Geordie a Form C3 for Customs Clearance in which Geordie had to declare, among other things, that he possessed no restricted goods (as if he'd admit it) and certifying that the items listed on the mysterious Bill of Lading were simply household effects. He certified, signed and returned the form.

Two weeks later on a sunny April morning, an articulated freight truck powered slowly up the long drive to Balnadarg between dense ranks of daffodils. It seemed incongruous to see such an enormous vehicle on a drive more accustomed to Land Rovers and farm vehicles. Geordie took his excited son, William, by the hand as they walked down the drive to instruct the vehicle driver where to unload its contents.

The driver was unexpectedly bolshie, "Didn't they tell yer, mate? You're supposed to unload this yourself. You've got 'alf an hour." He sounded like a male clone of Ms Buzzard. He jumped out of his cab and unfastened the awning on the side of the truck, revealing huge crates of effects for Geordie to lift off.

"There's no way I can shift this stuff."

"You've got 'alf an hour." The driver said flatly, clearly uninterested in lending a hand. "Sorry mate." He climbed back into the cab, poured himself a coffee from a silver thermos, looked pointedly at his watch and unfurled a copy of the Sun.

Josie procured four Polish farmworkers from a field nearby with the promise of a tip. They heaved and manhandled the crates off the truck onto the lawn. The lids were as tightly nailed as coffins. Fortunately it was a sunny day so there was no risk of spoilage. After

20 minutes the driver clambered down from his cab, refastened the awning on the side of the truck and handed Geordie a delivery note. "Sign 'ere, mate."

Geordie lifted an eyebrow, but signed. The driver tore off a copy, gave it to Geordie and stuffed the original in his top pocket. He drove off, leaving the Kinloch family and four Poles surrounded by crates on the lawn. The Poles hung around desultorily until Josie fetched her handbag and passed out a few banknotes.

"Well, I suppose I'd better get a claw-hammer and open these boxes up. Then we can move the stuff into the house."

"Ooh, can I help?" William asked excitedly.

"Of course you can."

"Right. Let's have a crack at this one." Geordie selected a wooden crate, roughly a cubic metre in size. He slid the claw under the lid. "Here you are, old chap, see if you can get it off."

The small boy hung off the hammer and pulled with all his might. Two nails squeaked slowly upwards. Geordie repositioned the hammer further along the lid and William repeated the process. Soon the lid was loose and with one final heave it creaked off. Inside, all that could be seen were wads of newspaper. A December 31 issue of The New York Post lay on top.

"Must be for padding." Geordie pulled out several layers of newspapers to see what was underneath. "Just more New York Posts. Hmm. Let's try another box." They repeated the process. More newspapers. And again, and again. Soon all the lids were off, propped up against the opened boxes. All filled with newspapers.

William began to cry. "I thought there would be toys and chairs and kettles in here. Why did you bring only newspapers back from America, Daddy?"

"I think they got our boxes muddled up, Willy. Don't worry, I'll call them and I'm sure they'll be delivered in the next day or so." But the wee fellow was inconsolable. He'd envisaged a cornucopia of shiny new things from America tumbling onto the lawn. Instead all he got was tons and tons of boring paper for the recycling skip.

Josie stood back, hands on hips, with a bit of a smirk. Geordie caught her eye. "Don't say a thing, Josie."

She didn't need to.

Chapter 10

The Literary Society

Like everybody – how he was sick of the expression – Geordie Kinloch 'had a book in him'. After countless late nights, arguments with his wife, the bewilderment of his children, astonishment of his parents, amusement of his friends and scepticism of his enemies, a manuscript was born. One witness of this titanic struggle was his old friend Father Saintey who observed fondly, '*parturiunt montes, nascetur mus.*' The mountains shook, a mouse was born.

Geordie was not content to tie a pink ribbon around his mouse, shove it in a drawer and rest content in the knowledge that he'd already accomplished more than the vast majority of wannabe writers. No, he wanted his manuscript published.

He asked around and someone came up with the name of a publisher in the North of England reputed to be sympathetic to first-time authors. Geordie called the man on the feeble pretext that he was passing through Hexham the next Thursday around two o'clock and wondered if he could drop by for a chat for half an hour.

"By all means. I'd be delighted to talk to you for half an hour at two o'clock next Thursday."

Geordie rose early. It was a glorious June morning. The rhododendrons and azaleas were in full scented bloom around the castle. The countryside was in wonderful heart for the 200 miles to Hexham. The trees were in their first pale green flush of growth and the Border lambs were fattening. He arrived in the area by late morning and had time to potter around the excavations at the nearby Roman fort of Vindolanda. He then drove to the centre of Hexham and munched on a sandwich in a public park until the hour came to 'drop by'.

He found the sign for HexLit Publishing in a narrow alleyway. He climbed up a steep, dingy staircase and into a long, low room that could best be described as a garret. Broken cardboard boxes lined the walls, loose books spilled haphazardly onto the floor and covered practically every flat surface in the room. But the place was surprisingly well lit, with open Velux rooflights letting in a pleasant breeze.

A slim girl with springy brown locks was on her knees trying to tidy a pile of books on the floor. From where he stood at the entrance Geordie couldn't help noticing that she wore no underwear. Her blouse was unbuttoned and her short black skirt rode up her thigh. She exuded a coltish, unconscious sexuality that was completely at odds with her colleague. He was an unshaven obese middle-aged man with long, thinning, grey, greasy hair, looming behind a Victorian desk submerged in papers. Geordie stepped over piles of books and stretched forward to shake his hand.

"How do you do, I'm Marvin Wainwright and this is my daughter Colette. Find us all right? Where did you just come from?" The man wheezed from the effort of standing up. Geordie marvelled at the genetic miracle which allowed this tub of lard to sire such a nymph.

"I was seeing some friends down in Yorkshire," Geordie lied. "I'm on my way to Scotland and you were en route. I appreciate you taking the time to see me. I thought it would be a good opportunity to introduce myself and show you my manuscript.'

"Absolutely delighted. What's it about?"

"Oh, it's the first of a trilogy about a young man sent away to board in Wales. First love, the death of his parents, bullying, a strange relationship with his Classics master, that kind of thing."

"Autobiographical?"

"Er . . . no . . . not at all. But obviously it contains episodes and situations that I might have observed over the course of my life." Geordie hated himself for fudging the answer. Barring the change of names, dates, places and a bit of literary licence thrown in, the book was massively autobiographical.

"Yes, quite." Wainwright said sceptically, "Can I see it?"

"Sure." Geordie handed over a heavy brown envelope containing 348 pages of his magnum opus. Wainwright weighed the package in his right hand.

"Chunky."

"I suppose so, but it takes time to develop the plot."

Wainwright didn't follow up on Geordie's explanation, but plunged right to the bottom line.

"I think I should tell you how we do things around here. The first thing we do is pass manuscripts out to our professional readers. We have a network of retired teachers and suchlike people dotted around the countryside in Northumberland. They have a good idea of what sells and what I like to publish. I should warn you that I only publish about one in twenty of the books my readers look at.'

"Low odds, but I'm confident," Geordie asserted hopefully.

"It's the same as music or painting. Only one song in twenty is worth listening to. Only one painting in twenty merits wasting your eyesight on . . . " He peered over his spectacles. Arching his eyebrows he fixed Geordie with a cynical expression, ". . . if that."

"Fair enough." Despite the man's shambolic demeanour Geordie quite liked Wainwright. Highly opinionated, but professionally he seemed incisive and organized. His daughter kept slotting books into piles on the floor, looking up to smile at Geordie from time to time. That blouse . . .

"To continue: if my reader likes a book, he or she will recommend that I should take it on. I will then read it and if I like it too, I will pass it to one of our editors. Like the readers, our editors are mainly retired teachers or university lecturers. They are ruthless in their approach to editing. Same as Ernest Hemingway, we believe that what makes a book great is the amount cut out in the editorial process. You'd be amazed how much fat you can cut from a book without affecting the muscle of the story."

"Do I have any say as to what gets edited? Assuming my book makes the cut, that is."

"Nice pun, squire. Nice pun. Tentatively, yes. If we like your book it's because we see commercial potential in it. If that means hacking it around because it'll enhance its commercial viability, then we'll hack it around. Of course we work closely with our writers, but often a writer doesn't like his work being heavily edited. In that case we shake hands and he goes his own way. No hard feelings. I'm glad to say that nobody who's left us in this manner has yet gone on to be successful with a book. Most of the books we take on will sell 10,000 to 15,000 copies, which is financially viable for us and moderately lucrative for the author. If we publish two a year for you, you can build a nice franchise."

"What's the timeframe for the whole publishing process?"

"You should allow six weeks for my readers to turn a manuscript around. They might be sitting on 10 or 12 manuscripts at any one time. God, I pity my readers. Ploughing through all that turgid middle-brow suburban crap would give me a permanent migraine." Wainwright held his head in his hands in mock agony. "Sorry, I digress." Wainwright saw Geordie arching an eyebrow. "If the reader likes your manuscript you should then give me a week to read it and decide whether to publish. I rarely turn a book down at this stage, but it's been known to happen. That's followed by the editorial process. Allow four weeks. Once the editing is finished we give the manuscript to a designer and layout expert to set up the book for publication. He's usually clogged up, so allow another four weeks. Then the printing and pre-publication hype — another four weeks, maybe. How many weeks is that?"

Geordie had been counting with his fingers. "Nineteen."

"OK, about five months, but to be on the safe side you should allow six, assuming the book proceeds normally. But we're getting ahead of ourselves. Don't be discouraged if we decide not to publish your book. It'll only be because it doesn't suit our house range. We'll wish you the very best and I'm sure it'll do well with the right publisher. Rejection's nothing to be ashamed of. Par for the course, actually. Apocryphal or not, the book world is full of stories of publishers who rejected writers like Nabokov and J.K. Rowling.

I have an antique dealer friend who missed buying a Bernini bust for £200 in a Clapham junkshop. While he was thinking about it over lunch another bloke spotted it and bought it. That bloke then sold it at auction for £2.2m."

"So where do we go from here?"

"I send this manuscript out to one of my readers and you wait." Marvin Wainwright dropped the package on his desk with a dusty thump. "For your peace of mind, I invite you to start pestering me at the end of August."

"OK," Geordie replied. "On the assumption that you like the book, what sort of financial deal do you strike up with your authors?"

"That's easy. They all get 15 per cent of the price that we, as publishers, achieve for the sale. For example, if the book sells in a shop for £10 and after the bookseller's cut I get £6 per book, you get 15 percent of six quid, which is 90 pence. Even if it's massively discounted or the bookseller is particularly greedy — which they often are — you will get 15 per cent of whatever I get. I try to keep it very simple. I pay royalties quarterly on the basis of my receipts. The sales figures are independently audited."

"Do you pay an advance?"

"Never. If the book's successful you do well. If it does badly we're quits. I'm too small to take the risk of shelling out advances to authors."

"Fair enough."

"If you manage to navigate successfully around all these hurdles and we publish your book, are you available to help promoting it?"

"I'll make myself as available as it takes. I'm dead keen to make a success of this venture. I'd be thrilled if you arranged a book signing tour. Will you arrange press reviews?"

"Up to a point. We're reasonably well-connected with the major dailies and the Sunday newspapers, but the odds are not good. I understand that over 80,000 new fiction titles come out each year in the UK. Fewer than 3000 sell more than a thousand copies. In crude terms that means there are 77,000 new titles floating around in the wilderness, which nobody wants to buy. My point is that it's very hard to grab the attention of an influential reviewer who'll take the time to read a new author and do any write-up in the national press, let alone produce a good write-up. The odds are stacked heavily against you."

"I know a few people I could contact who'd give me a decent review, I'm sure. I was at school with Richard Royds, for example."

"Richard Royds, no less? Well, if you got him to review your book you'd be ahead of the game. Have you kept in touch with him?"

"Not exactly, but I'm sure he'll remember me. We ran the school Literary Society together. We were quite close friends in those days."

"Well, once we've gone through the vetting process and if we decide to publish you, it would be good for you to contact Richard Royds and get him to write a pre-publication review. That would be worth a few thousand copies right there."

"Only if it's a good review."

"Obviously."

Geordie motored North with a light heart. Whether his meeting with the corpulent Mr Wainwright would come to fruition or not, he felt pleased and relieved. He had taken the initiative to arrange an adult conversation with a real publisher who was now going to seriously consider his book. Despite the wall of scepticism from Geordie's family over the project, Wainwright seemed to be taking him seriously and intended to give him a fair hearing. He was bound to, of course. Geordie might just be the next Dickens or Turgenev or, who knows, Ian Fleming.

He wondered how to get hold of Richard Royds. If he sent a letter through his publisher it would surely get lost amidst the daily sackloads of fan mail. He could try contacting Royds through the school. They must surely be keeping tabs on their most distinguished alumni. The school was not noted for high achievers. To have produced a boy who not only got eight O levels and four A levels, and then won a place at Cambridge to study English Lit. was exceedingly rare in the history of the school.

Richard Royds also happened to be a pretty boy at school, quite the Adonis, so no one was likely to forget him. Everyone was a bit in love with Ricky, although as far as Geordie knew he escaped the place with his virtue intact. No question, the school would definitely know where he was. For all he knew the governors had already erected a bust of him in the school commons.

When he returned to Balnadarg that evening, Geordie wrote a letter to the school Registrar asking for the address of their distinguished former pupil and his great old friend, Richard Royds. He pointed out that he was well aware of the Data Protection Act but he was certain his dear friend would be delighted to have his address passed on.

Two weeks later he received a curt letter from the Registrar to the effect that he could find no record of Geordie having been a pupil there, and, sorry, but who was Richard Royds?

Eventually he tracked down the friend of a mutual friend who had spotted Richard Royds fairly recently. Geordie received an address, with strict instructions not to divulge who had given it to him. He composed his letter.

Dear Ricky,
I hope you don't mind me making contact with you after all this time. You'll probably be surprised to hear from me. I've been watching your literary successes with admiration (yes, and a certain amount of envy) over the years. I particularly enjoyed The Ocean Sweep. Congratulations – brilliant, evocative stuff.

I know you're a very busy man so I'll get right to the point. Do you remember fantasizing in the Literary Society at school about all those novels we were going to write? Well, you beat me to it but I have finally managed to produce one. I've just left a manuscript with a publisher who is making encouraging noises.

The publisher told me that it would significantly enhance my chance of success if I got some good pre-publishing reviews.

Recalling our long evenings in the school library I thought you might be good enough to read the MS and give me a few positive words that could be written on the front cover. Something like, 'This book is a breathtaking journey through the landscape of the past. I simply couldn't put it down.' You know, that kind of thing.

I won't burden you with the manuscript just now. But if you agree to read it I will send it to you by return. Again, I hope you don't mind my contacting you after all these years. For all I know you have atrocious memories of our school days and don't want to be reminded. But with the hope that you would enjoy a reunion, I look forward to hearing from you.

All the best,
Geordie (Kinloch)

THE LITERARY SOCIETY

Life went on at Balnadarg. It was an unusually wet summer and Geordie was preoccupied on the land. In mid-August he was thrilled to hear that HexLit's reader had recommended to Marvin Wainwright that they should take his book further. His literary ball was rolling nicely along. It gave him the confidence to start work on the second volume of the trilogy, in anticipation of massive public demand for it after the first was published. One morning in early September a letter arrived for him.

Dear Geordie Kinloch
Richard Royds thanks you for your letter.
He is flattered that you have such a high opinion of him and grateful that you have been buying and reading his books. However, he has a policy not to write reviews for unknown writers in response to unsolicited letters. You will appreciate that an author of his standing receives many similar communications, and that he cannot possibly deal with them all personally.
I enclose a brochure that sets out Richard Royds's itinerary for the next two months as he promotes his latest best-seller. His itinerary should take him to a bookshop near you and I expect he will be pleased to meet you at the book signing.
Yours faithfully
Marie Jacques
for
Richard Royds

Geordie opened the brochure of Richard Royds's itinerary. It looked like a rock band's world tour. The locations were not exactly Wembley Stadium, but the literary equivalent. He was booked to appear at a number of major Borstones outlets throughout the country. He was scheduled for 16 in London alone.
Borstones dominated retail book distribution in the UK. Writers

who had their seal of approval were virtually guaranteed massive sales. This meant a nice income stream, despite the fact that Borstones kept 50 per cent of the retail price for selling a book.

Geordie noted that Dick Royds's itinerary would be taking him to Borstones in Edinburgh for a reading and book signing evening in early October in four weeks' time. He called Marvin Wainwright.

"Good news! My old friend Richard Royds will be in Edinburgh for a book reading and signing at Borstones on October 5th. Is there any chance that my book will be printed by then? It would be great to give him a copy to review."

"That should be possible Geordie. Are you confident he'll write something for you?"

"Confident? He and I spent five of the most impressionable years of our lives together at school. We were in the same class. We studied together, played rugger and tennis together. We used to go off and smoke a fag in the trees from time to time. We co-founded and ran the Literary Society. So, yes, I'm confident he'll write a few words of support for my book."

"That's great then. What we'll do is run up a decent proof copy and you can give it to him. We'll wait to print the cover. How long do you think it'll take him to review the book?"

"It shouldn't take him long. A weekend, maybe. I'll ask a special favour."

"I'm glad you're such a close friend of our greatest living novelist." Geordie missed Wainwright's sarcasm. "When his review comes out we'll incorporate it on the front cover, do a quick print run and attach the covers to the book. Looks like we might need to do a print run of 15,0000–20,0000 to meet demand."

"Then you'll have to organize a Borstones tour for me around the British Isles, won't you?" Geordie laughed, still mistaking Wainwright's tone.

Geordie recalled his adolescent escapades with Ricky Royds, the sweet peachy scent of the yellow gorse flowers behind the playing fields, the skylarks twittering high in the air as the boys lay smoking Balkan Sobranie Cocktails in the grass. He remembered Ricky distinctly saying that one day he'd be the greatest living novelist, and Geordie replying, 'No – you'll be the second greatest living novelist.' He'd never forgotten Ricky's generous reply: 'In that case it will be my honour to be the best friend of the greatest living novelist.' Thirty years earlier.

Geordie wrote another letter, this time by way of Marie Jacques.

Dear Ricky,
This is to let you know that I will be at your soiree at Borstones in Edinburgh on October 5th. May I invite you to dinner afterwards at the Oyster Bar of the Café Royal? I'd like to give you the book I mentioned in my last letter for you to review. I look forward immensely to catching up with you.
À bientôt
Geordie

No response came, even from the redoubtable Marie Jacques. Geordie was not unduly concerned, knowing that Ricky was in the throes of a heavy promotion schedule around the UK.

A proof copy of Geordie's novel arrived at Balnadarg on the first day of October. The family was thrilled. Even Josie was impressed by his determination to see through the project. The children invited friends over to admire the book with their father's name on it. They weren't allowed to touch it. Geordie picked it up from time to time and flicked through its pages with a very real sense of satisfaction. This was his first step in a new life.

October 5th was overcast from beginning to end. By early evening it began to rain steadily. Geordie had trouble parking anywhere close to the bookshop in Edinburgh. He was soaked by the time he arrived at Borstones. The entrance was mobbed. It was even too crowded for umbrellas. Geordie was drenched and tried to work his way through the crowd, but it became denser the further into the shop he pushed. He asked a woman what the crowds were all about. She replied, "Richard Royds is coming here tonight for a book reading and signing."

"This crowd's for him?" Geordie replied incredulously, jerking his thumb into the shop. "Where is he?"

"He's at the back of the shop somewhere. He should be speaking in a few minutes."

"Well, that'll be a treat." Geordie muscled his way as far forward as he could and positioned himself in a corner with as good a view of the podium as he could find. A hunched man with a receding hairline sat at a wide table, signing books at the head of an excited queue. He asked mechanically, 'Who for?' as each copy slid in front of him. 'To Doris, with Love'?' He slid the book back across the table and slid a new one forward. 'Who for?'

Eventually a tough-looking woman in a pink dress tapped a microphone at the table. "Good evening, everybody. We are delighted that you made the effort to come out on such a miserable evening to be present at the launch of Rick's latest novel in Edinburgh. Please feel free to help yourselves to a glass of wine at the table in the back, and buy as many books as you like for Rick to sign. Borstones have laid on a huge supply for this evening's launch. Without further ado I'd like to hand over to our greatest living author."

Someone shouted "Wa Hae Ricky." Royds nodded and stood up.

Geordie was struck by how tired and paunchy he looked. He had heavy bags under the eyes — doubtless the result of a lifetime of late nights writing in poor light.

"Edinburgh is the literary lion's den," he began, to applause and more Wa Haes, "and I am privileged to be here today in the city of Robert Louis Stevenson, Rankin, Conan Doyle and J.K. Rowling. As some of you know, I am three-quarters Scottish. When my family came home from India my Edinburgh Grandmother was our anchor in this country. As children she took us to the zoo, to Arthur's Seat, to the Botanics and to all the art galleries. I feel more than rooted in this city, and I thank you for your welcome.

My latest book is a departure from my usual themes. It is set in the Battle of Passchendaele in 1917 and is about the love between two men who are doomed to die in the mud."

Royds described his motivation for writing the book, read a few paragraphs of vivid prose and thanked the audience for attending his launch party. He concluded, "I'm afraid I have to go to Glasgow tonight. I've left a pile of signed books for those of you who were not able to have a personalized message written by me. Good night, everyone."

The lady in pink ushered him from the table and through an emergency exit at the back of the store, and they were gone. Geordie hadn't even got close to his old friend. He was reduced to being jostled among hundreds of groupies.

The next morning, Geordie called Marvin Wainwright and explained what had happened. Wainwright was silent for a moment, then answered.

"I was rather hoping that you might be one of the 3000 novelists to sell over a thousand this year. I'll tell the printers to keep you to 500 copies."

"I'm sure that Rick will do a review for me."

"Let's see how the 500 copies do first, shall we?"

Chapter 11

Niki's Love

Geordie had the sad task of clearing up his father's effects after he died. His affairs were well organized, tabbed and filed. Geordie found only one item which bore no explanation. In a Florentine leather cufflink box was an oval aluminium dog-tag perforated along the middle. Engraved on each side of the perforation was 90pzG D Ahren.

In homage to his father's memory he set himself the task of going through his address book and contacting as many of his old friends as he could. After one phone session he arranged to meet Eddie Watson at a pub in Corbridge the following Saturday.

The old chap loosened up after a pint of Starbright. It turned out that he'd trained with Geordie's father 'up the road in Otterburn' and they'd fought the Germans together in Africa and Sicily. "Then we invaded Italy. It was a bloody business. We ended the war dancing in a fountain in Padua, if I remember rightly. We left a lot of our friends behind." Eddie fell silent.

Geordie leaned across the table and showed him the dog-tag. "What do you make of this, Eddie? I found it in my father's stuff."

Eddie studied it. "It's a German dog-tag, a soldier's identification disc. 90pzG would be the 90th Panzer Grenadier division. They held the German lines opposite us at the end of the war. D Ahren is probably the name of the chap who bought it."

"Do you have any memory of who he might be?"

"D'you know, thousands of Germans died in the final days of the war. Could be any one of them. Can't help you there, I'm afraid."

As he drove north through the wild Border lands, Geordie tried to imagine who D Ahren might have been.

The culture prevailing in Germany in 1944 was possibly the foulest ever witnessed in the world. It was indefensible, but it must be recognized that vast numbers of innocent, decent German people were dragged into the gears of the Führer's threshing machine. They were separated from what they loved, sliced, diced and boxed into units according to skills, experience and fighting capability then parcelled into whatever role most suited Hitler's purpose.

European opinion is still astonished years after the event and often asks: Why didn't they stand up to the system? If enough Germans had resisted, none of this would have happened. By definition, this is absolutely true. But many did resist in a piecemeal way and paid a horrible price. The Reich had a place for them: they found their way to Gestapo torture cells, mass graves at Buchenwald or penal battalions on the Russian Front.

By late 1944 the military draft age in Germany and its occupied territories was widened to include all males aged from 16 to 60. Even boys of 14 who volunteered were not turned away. They were given basic training and sent to bolster one of three sagging fronts: the Eastern Front, to hold back the savage Russian hordes, the Western Front, to resist the well-supplied American and British armies, or the Home Front, to fire flak into the sky and pull charred corpses from the ruins of fire-stormed cities throughout Germany.

Dolf was a boy from the pretty village of Assmanshausen on the Rhine. He had been an undistinguished student at the local gymnasium and reached his 16th birthday in December 1944. His mother prayed fervently that the war would finish before he was conscripted into the Wehrmacht. Dolf prayed hesitantly that he would get the chance to see some action — but not too much. In defiance of his mother's prayers that her beautiful flaxen boy would be overlooked in the *fin-de-guerre* turmoil, Dolf received his call-up papers on the very eve of his birthday. He was ordered to take the military transport to

Koblenz and present himself at the local RAD – Reichsarbeitsdienst, or Labour Service – barracks for basic training.

At the beginning of the war basic infantry training in the German army was a three-month affair, followed by a further three months of specialist training. Recruits were typically inducted into the RAD, where they learned the basic trade of war. It included digging ditches, constructing fortifications, erecting barbed wire, basic weaponry and incessant square bashing. As in most armies the inculcation of blind obedience was the core objective of basic military training. Every recruit was observed closely for his skills and soldier-worthiness, after which he was sent for further training to his allocated cadre. It might be the Panzers, the Luftwaffe or even a non-combat role in logistics or engineering.

By 1945 the training process had contracted to a two-week crash-course. On his first day Dolf was given seven inoculations — he lost count after tetanus. The boys drilled with shovels because there were no rifles and in their civilian clothes because there were no uniforms. The training sergeant marched the recruits at the double through the bombed streets of Koblenz wearing gas masks, carrying 80 pounds of equipment on their backs. Boys dropped like flies. The sudden, violent training that followed years of malnutrition and innocence was enough to kill many of the schoolchildren.

At the beginning of the second week Dolf's platoon was taught by a legless veteran of the Crete Campaign how to strip, clean and operate a Spandau machine gun, a service rifle and a light mortar. They were lectured on the iron principles of military discipline, assured that the Führer was immensely proud of them and sent south by cattle truck through Austria into Italy.

The train suffered interminable delays caused by Allied air raids. A dozen times the locomotive stopped, the unteroffizier barked, exhausted young soldiers shouldered their equipment, leaped off the railway wagons and dispersed into ditches and surrounding fields. Mostly these were 'training evacuations', they were told. Three times the train was strafed by patrolling Hurricanes and Mustangs. Carriages were shot up, equipment destroyed and many young men mangled by cannon fire. But miraculously the train remained on its tracks until it reached its destination.

They were kicked out of the cattle wagon at eleven o'clock on the third night. In the darkness Dolf fell in with his platoon and stumbled across a bomb-ravaged freight yard. He did not know, nor was he told, where he was. Padua, someone said. Who knew? In baggy, stained, second-hand uniform and lugging his scarred battle-salvaged equipment he was transferred to a truck hauling other conscripted boys and material to the Gothic Line.

The convoy was met four hours later, after many further stops and alarms, by a group of stretcher-bearers and a crowd of surly, unkempt Italian non-combatants. A German NCO supervised the rapid offloading of supplies from the vehicles. Stretchers of wounded men were lifted aboard some trucks; German corpses were piled onto others. The trucks needed to be turned round and concealed along the road behind the lines as quickly as possible. If they were still driving at first light they would be destroyed by predatory Hurricane pilots stalking the route on dawn patrol.

The fresh troops were ordered to load boxes of ammunition and food into panniers mounted on the flanks of pack animals. Dolf stroked the soft muzzle of a donkey as it stood patiently being loaded up.

"Don't worry, my little friend. It'll be over soon and you can go back to your pasture among the buttercups." The animal's ears flickered in a momentary acknowledgement of unaccustomed kindness.

"Hey, you great booby, leave that donkey alone. Catch this". A 30kg wooden case of artillery shells was thrust into his arms. Dolf staggered under the weight but was determined not to show weakness. He hauled it onto the donkey's back and strapped it down.

"I think he's fully loaded now, sir." Dolf volunteered to the NCO. He had noticed the donkey's hind legs buckling as it took the weight.

"He's loaded when I say he's loaded. What's your name, boy?"

"Dolf, sir."

"That's not a name in the German Army."

"Dolf Ahren, sir" He could make out the thin, weary face of the NCO in the weak torchlight. It wasn't a bad face, just one that had seen everything. A face that Dolf knew not to trifle with.

"Very well, Ahren. If you're worried about that fella, put just another half load of shells on his back, and the other half on your back. Then get ready and follow me. We need to be in the mountains before dawn otherwise we'll be caught napping by the RAF."

Dolf found his kit and rifle and strapped the shell-box to the top of his pack. The platoon of unseasoned troops formed up alongside the convoy of heavily laden donkeys and began trudging uphill along a rough track, exhausted before they started.

"Ahren, you will realize very quickly that in war there is no room for compassion." The NCO shouted from behind him in the darkness. "If you get another person, or another creature, to do your work for you, then you should do so. Mark my words, within 500 paces you will wish that you hadn't felt sentimental about that donkey." Dolf smiled weakly to himself at the NCO's words, relieved by the conciliatory tone in his voice. He felt stupid for earlier showing a sign of weakness by stroking the donkey.

"Yes sir, I won't make that mistake again." he said, determined to get to their destination without admitting he was being crushed by the extra weight. He was a soldier now, and German soldiers did not complain.

The track steepened and roughened. The journey seemed endless as Dolf stumbled to keep alongside his donkey. A mile ahead in the hills, the landscape was momentarily lit by flashes from explosions and punctuated by the rat-tat-tat of machine guns. In the staccato flashes Dolf saw the line of donkeys and soldiers ascending the mountain track ahead of him.

He gripped the pannier on the donkey's flank, allowing it to tug him uphill and saving him from falling out from exhaustion. The weight of his pack, rifle, ammunition and extra shells made it difficult to lift his legs. The canvas straps cut into his shoulders. The convoy plodded into a biting wind. He was as tired as he had ever been. He was hungry. He had no idea where he was, but for stroboscopic flashes from the shell fire illuminating the rough stone terraces hewn into the hillside.

"Halt and unload! We have a very short time to deploy this material." A streak of light in the wintry eastern sky heralded the end of 12 hours' January darkness. Dolf wondered where he would sleep, when he would eat. He dared not ask. He dropped his pack and unloaded the donkey's panniers. Some animals were remounted immediately with wounded men, others had corpses slung and secured over their backs with rope, like rugs. The uncomplaining donkeys were turned around by their Italian drivers and led downhill again.

"Men, welcome to the battle zone. Leave all material on the ground beside you, take your packs, ammunition and rifles and follow me. Keep your heads down and be quiet." Dolf formed up behind a line of other recruits and they were led further uphill for half a mile. They were deployed among olive trees around the edge of a plateau.

"Men, I suggest you take this opportunity to rest. You have one hour. Soup and bread will be provided by the field kitchen at 7 o'clock, then Hauptmann Johannes will be here at 7.15 to give your orders for the day."

Dolf curled under an ilex tree. Despite the intense cold he closed his eyes and descended rapidly into sleep. His mother was cooking thick soup in the warm kitchen. The cat lay on the windowsill in the sunshine. Niki called for him. They ran through the vineyards above the village. They lay on their stomachs watching barges chugging into the current of the Rhine far below. Her hair blew across his face, their laughing blue eyes were electric with love.

"*Schnell, schnell,* form up." Dolf was booted on the backside. "Hauptmann Johannes will address the new arrivals in two minutes." Dolf shot to his feet, to see the field kitchen being hunkered into a trench for the day. He had missed the only opportunity for food on either side of 24 hours.

"Men, welcome to the Gothic Line. You are now with the 90th Panzer-Grenadier Division, charged with the critical task of holding a line which the Wehrmacht has held for many months." A volley of bullets cracked overhead and smacked into the olive trees a few feet above the hauptmann's head. He didn't flinch, but grimaced as the frightened recruits picked themselves off the ground.

"Your orders are to protect a battery of six 75mm *leichtes infantriegeschutz* mountain guns deployed on the hillside behind us." Dolf peered uphill but saw nothing among the trees, terraces and boulders. Bullets were singing off the rocks, accompanied by the repetitive crash of mortar shells straddling the mountainside.

"You will be positioned in picket positions down the hill and you must meet all advances with immediate resistance. You will open fire immediately on sight of the enemy and hold your positions at all cost. Every minute you hold back the English infantry will enable our artillery to find their range and annihilate them." As he turned he patted Dolf on the shoulder. With an expression of unfathomable sadness, the hauptmann turned away and scrambled uphill back towards his hidden guns.

A corporal led the recruits downhill, deploying them singly

behind this rock, that tree or in the lee of a ruined mountain hut. He positioned Dolf beside an ancient hump-backed stone bridge. It carried a goat path across a mountain stream. "Watch this path like a hawk and shoot anyone coming up the hill. Hold this position until you are relieved, or . . . " The corporal's sentence tapered off.

"What's your name, boy?"

"Dolf Ahren, sir."

"Good luck, Dolf Ahren. Make the Führer proud of you."

"Yes, sir."

Dolf threw himself on the ground as a surge of shellfire screamed overhead. The corporal laughed, "That's outgoing, Dolf Ahren. From our own guns – the guns you are here to protect."

"Yes, sir." He remembered his father once talking about the shellfire at Verdun, how it howled like an express train overhead. Dolf would now have something to talk about to his children one day.

Dolf hid along the shallow parapet of the bridge on the uphill side, commanding an uninterrupted field of fire over the winding path below. He loaded his rifle, slid the chamber bolt, placed ammunition in a neat pile beside him and waited, tense as a panther.

The skirmishing ceased and the mountain fell silent. The air warmed as the sun rose. A thrush sang enchantingly in the trees below, the stream burbled busily. As the action died down, Dolf's attention eased. He trailed his fingers in the icy water and splashed his face to wash off the grime of three nights' travelling in a cattle truck. Focusing on the path below and listening intently, he slipped his steel helmet off and loosened his collar. Holding his breath, he plunged his head into the pool, scrubbing the filth out of his hair and neck. A few seconds later, much refreshed, he resumed the sniper's position. He stared intently along the barrel of the rifle, helmet on the ground beside him as his flaxen hair dried in the winter sun.

Like a summer thunderstorm the battle seemed to blow away

from his sector, occasionally erupting in ever-more distant claps of shellfire far to the west. Dolf wondered whether any comrades were deployed nearby. He shouted in the direction the corporal had walked three hours earlier, "Hello, is anyone else on the mountain?" Silence. "I'm so hungry. How long before I move from this position?" Silence. "I'm so tired. When do I sleep?" More silence. Was he being watched? Was he being tested? He had to obey orders or he would be shot for disobedience. What if they had forgotten him? Should he rejoin his unit? No – he was a forward picket of the 90th Panzer-Grenadier Division. He was here to provide an early alarm against the advancing English army, hold them back at all cost.

Niki returned to his thoughts in a pang of excitement. How he missed her . . . how she would love it here in the Italian sunshine by this ancient bridge. He peeled a piece of dripping moss off a rock in the stream and pressed the green sponge to his lips. "My Darling Niki, when I return from the war we will be together forever and ever more." He smiled, wondering what she might be doing at exactly this moment in Assmanshausen. It was lunchtime. Lunchtime! She would be helping her mother in the hostel, ladling soup to those poor orphaned children evacuated from Köln. He pictured her long slim legs, those lovely hands, her white teeth, her smiling oval face. Her kisses, those sweet, sweet kisses.

He lay in the sunshine with his cheek resting on the rifle, eyes closed but ready to spring to action if the corporal returned or the English arrived. He would put on his helmet in a flash. He was the very soul of vigilance. Niki took his hand and they walked up their bluff overlooking the Rhine. It was a brilliant blue day, swallows screamed and skimmed just above the vines before soaring into the summer sky. Church bells tolled, a dog barked. She loosened the buttons of her shirt, guided his hand to her breasts. Her eyes locked with his, their lips parted.

"Here's one, surr."

Dolf sprang from his reverie to the thump of footsteps. He grabbed his rifle and turned to see a kilted Highland soldier lunging at him. "*Nein, nein Kamarad!*" Dolf put up his arms in appeasement as the flashing bayonet plunged into his liver. For a moment he smiled at the Scot, as if to say, "You wouldn't really do that, would you?", then buckled in agony as the wiry soldier put a boot on his chest to pull out the bayonet. Dolf convulsed as blood spurted from his uniform. He fell backwards, stone dead, and came to rest with his head hanging over the stream. Blood poured from his mouth, matting his hair, a crimson stain mingling in the icy water and vanishing downstream.

"Well done, McRitchie. You got the bastard before he got us." The subaltern praised the Highlander as he wiped the blood off his bayonet on Dolf's trousers.

"Aye – focking Hitler Youth. The only guid Nazi's a dead Nazi, surr."

"Come on, men, watch out for other snipers hiding in these terraces." The platoon of Highlanders pressed on up the hill.

Later that afternoon, the German guns were put out of action and the day's objectives were secured. Major Kinloch hiked up to the Highlanders' new bivouac for a tactical assessment of the next day's action. On the way he stopped at a quaint stone bridge. He noticed a young blond German lying dead below the parapet, spread-eagled over the rocks. His head hung backwards, just above the stream; one hand dangled in the water, his fingers blue and stiff in the glacial flow.

"Sergeant, give me a hand to pull this chap off the rocks and lay him out with more dignity. He's only a boy."

"Yes, surr." They laid Dolf's body beside the bridge, kicked his small pile of ammunition into the stream, disabled his rifle and stuck it, bayonet first, into the stony soil. They placed the oversized

German helmet atop Dolf's rifle, marking the site for a salvage team to deal with later. Major Kinloch kneeled silently by the body of the young soldier in his comically large uniform. He noticed the small oval aluminium army dog tag around his neck. 90pz D Ahren was engraved on each side of a perforated line. He lifted it off the boy's neck and put it in his pocket.

"You know, sergeant, he couldn't have been more than 16 years old. Same age as my brother. What a bitch this war is."

"Aye, surr, it's a bitch a'right."

As the pair continued uphill, Major Kinloch was unusually silent. The sergeant cast anxious sidelong glances at him.

"Are you all right, surr?"

"Yes, thank you, Sergeant," he answered tersely. "I've just got something in my eye."

Chapter 12

The Swallow

The tiny figure in a Shetland cardigan sat slumped in a chair in the corner of the common room. She was asleep, head lolling like a doll's, mouth open, her gaunt hollow cheeks belying the vital woman she used to be. Geordie sat opposite her in the window alcove, reading a newspaper while he waited. She eventually nodded awake in confusion, shouting in dismay for the other patients to hear – if only they could.

"Who are you? How did you get into my house?" she demanded angrily.

"Sshhh. It's me. Geordie. This isn't your house, it's a nursing home. I've come to visit you."

"Why are you here at breakfast time? How did you get into my house?"

"I came through the front door, past the Reception Desk. It's not breakfast time. It's four o'clock in the afternoon, tea time."

"I haven't had breakfast. You mustn't creep up on me like that." Observing the other folks slumped around the common room in various states of stupefaction, she demanded bluntly, "What are they doing in my house? I didn't invite them here."

"They're your friends, Daisy." Geordie spoke gently to his great aunt. She'd been part of Balnadarg for nearly 90 years, a golden thread woven through the lives of three generations of Kinlochs. "They live here too – don't you remember?"

She cocked her head, indicating that he'd spoken into her deaf ear.

"Live here too?" Her sense of time and space was shot to pieces.

"Yes Daisy. You share this place with your friends."

"Oh." Her eyes closed again.

He found it difficult to equate her skeletal husk with the rich memories she'd planted in him as a young boy. He would always remember the early mornings when she pottered busily around the pantry, baking Lorne sausage rolls. Geordie, wakened by the smell, would bounce out of bed and run down to the kitchen. The scent of sausage rolls always meant that an adventure was in the offing.

"Good morning, Geordie. It's my birthday today. We're going on an expedition to celebrate." Or, "Good morning, Geordie. It's St Andrew's Day. I'm taking you to St Andrews." Or she would simply announce a mystery jape for the fun of it.

They would be taken by the rattling post bus to a distant village in the glens. After hiking up a windswept corrie they would sit in their waterproofs atop a granite ridge, backs to the driving rain, eat the sausage rolls and drink lemon barley water. "The Queen drinks lemon barley water, you know. That's why she has such a beautiful complexion." After exploring a waterfall and pitying the poor sheep sheltering from the weather, they would catch the bus on its return trip and reach home two hours later. They were drenched to the marrow, but sublimely happy.

These experiences were tumbled in the pool of time, building sinews of strength and love into his troubled boyhood. Indeed, he never recaptured the sense of pure fun, even in the most glamorous resorts in exquisite company in later life, as when he sat with Great Aunt Daisy on a howling Highland outcrop munching sausage rolls as a six-year-old.

She stirred. Her eyes reopened and light returned to her furrowed face. "Goodness, how long have you been sitting there?" Her false teeth clacked.

"Just a few minutes, Daisy". Geordie was lucky this time. Sometimes he visited for half an hour and her eyes didn't open while he waited. He would leave quietly, hoping that his love would somehow flow into her as if by osmosis.

"How are you? What have you been up to?" he asked.

"Oh I've been terribly busy doing housework and gardening, some shopping too. I took McTaggart for a long walk in the woods this morning." McTaggart was her Scottie dog. He had died before Geordie was born.

"I'm glad you're keeping busy."

"Yes. Very busy, though I find it depressing about all these people who've moved into my house." She flicked her hand petulantly in the direction of three catatonic old dears slumped before a TV gardening programme. "They won't let me have a say in running things any more."

"This isn't your house, Daisy. You're in a nursing home. You'd be a lot happier if you just sat back and enjoyed yourself. You should enjoy the peace and quiet."

"They knocked my house down and built this place on top of the rubble."

"Really?"

"Yes, I know that because the view from here is exactly the same as the view from our old house. They took my paintings and hung them on the walls here." She pointed at a ghastly mass-produced engraving of Loch Lomond. "Be sure to take them when you go, won't you?" she whispered conspiratorially. "I've got some very good art, you know."

Geordie walked out of the nursing home feeling hollow. Nesting rooks cawed noisily in the Scots pines by the car park, evoking distant childhood summers in the Highlands. They reminded him of the rookery in the pines on the path to the Spey from Daisy's cottage, a heart-achingly long time ago.

He was greeted at Balnadarg by William belting along the

corridor with his arms open. Geordie scooped up his three-year-old son and hugged him tightly.

"What have you been up to, my little monkey?"

"I went in a helicopter today. High in the sky."

"You did? What did you see?"

"I saw our house. And zebras and soldiers."

"Really? That sounds fun. Did they say anything to you?"

"No. It was a helicopter. It made too much noise to hear what they said."

"I see."

Josie was in the drawing room surrounded by piles of paper, sorting notes for a book she was researching.

"How was Daisy?"

"Disconnected. We have to take it from one day to the next. I don't think she has long to go. She's incredibly frail now."

William wriggled in his arms.

"William was telling me about his helicopter today. What's that all about?"

"Oh – an army helicopter landed on the Back Hill this morning. Soldiers jumped out in the heather, let off some flares, fired a few guns, climbed back in and flew away. William saw the whole thing from his bedroom window and hasn't spoken about anything else since."

"Commandos training for mountain warfare, no doubt. So, William, tell me more about your helicopter."

"It was like a spaceship and men jumped out. I went there and they took me into the sky."

Geordie sat down on a sofa with William on his knee, coaxing him into nonsensical exaggerations about things he'd seen from the helicopter, encouraging him to make more and more outlandish claims.

"And you saw Balnadarg from the air?"

"Oh yes, I saw Ballydarg. The flag was flying."

As his son warbled excitedly about the marvels he had witnessed, Geordie hatched a plan.

Two days later he drove with William to the nursing home. He parked the car and took the excited boy by the hand.

"We're going to see Daisy."

"Daisy's a hundred years old," the small boy announced solemnly.

"Not quite. Another few years yet."

As they approached Reception, a nurse stopped Geordie. "Hello Mr Kinloch, I'm Eileen, the senior shift nurse. I just want you to know that we're getting quite concerned about Miss Kinloch. She's becoming increasingly confused and incoherent. She thinks she's in her own house and that we're her staff."

"Why do you think this is happening?"

"As you know she was diagnosed with Alzheimer's a while ago. This could be a sign that the disease is progressing. We need to keep a close watch on her. I just thought you should know."

Daisy was sitting in the common room, wide awake, staring at the feathery spring leaves on the trees outside and the quiet road beyond. Her face lit up when she saw Geordie and William.

"Hello, and who are you?" She always played the same game with her favourite child of her favourite great nephew.

"I'm William, silly." He cuddled her, adding, "I was in a helicopter yesterday."

"How very funny. I flew away on a swallow's back yesterday."

"What's a swallow?"

"It's a bird that comes in the summer."

"How did you get onto it, Aunt Daisy?"

"It flew into my room and I climbed on its back."

"Well I flew above Ballydarg and saw a zebra."

"Did you, now?" Daisy was charmed by the boy's imagination.

"Yes, it was running."

"You know, William, I remember when a zebra fell into the moat, a long, long time ago."

"I saw it falling in the moat too from the helicopter."

Turning to Geordie, she spoke sharply, "I told you the moat was dangerous. You must really see that it's fenced off before we have any other accidents." Geordie didn't have a clue what she was talking about. He patted the back of her bony hand, interlaced with ancient veins. It was black and blue from punctures caused by drip-needles.

"Yes, Daisy, don't worry. I'll see to it."

"What else did you take on the swallow's back?" William probed Daisy's imagination.

"Some fruit."

"Were there any bananas?"

"Oh yes, bananas. Come to think of it, I saw one falling out. It fell on a zebra."

Geordie loved listening to the good-humoured gibberish that flowed between the youngest and oldest members of his family. The two were separated by 95 years, yet seemed to meet squarely in the middle of a fantasy world. The Kinlochs were slow breeders. Geordie was a middle-aged bridge connecting the geriatric rambling of his great aunt with the infantile nonsense of his child.

"Then the zebra fell in the moat." William embellished the story.

Daisy became agitated again. She turned to Geordie "You really must see to the moat. That's the second zebra to fall in this morning, you know."

"No, it's the same zebra. Only one zebra fell in the moat," William insisted excitedly. "Only one, Aunt Daisy."

Geordie didn't have the agility to add to the surreal flow of conversation, but played along: "Daisy, can you remind me where the moat is?"

"It's outside, right there. Look, they're digging it out. You can see the flags." She pointed towards a line of orange traffic cones, cordoning off a stretch of the nursing home car park. Two men hung about lazily, smoking cigarettes. A shallow trench had been dug in the tarmac; a prelude, perhaps, to cables or a new waterpipe being laid. The scene did not exactly radiate energy.

"I do wish they'd hurry up or the moat'll never be finished."

"At least the zebras won't fall in, Daisy, will they?"

"That's true. At least the zebras won't fall in."

"I'm three, Aunt Daisy. I'll be four soon. Will you take me on your swallow for a treat?"

"We'll see." She ran the back of her hand over the contours of his beaming face in a gesture of supreme affection. "Swallows don't usually fly with two people. I'll have to speak to Guard."

"Who's Guard?"

"Guard watches over us. He sees everything. He knows what you're thinking, all the time. He never forgets."

William clapped his hands. "Did Guard see that?"

"Guard sees everything. He even knows what you're going to do tomorrow."

"What am I going to do tomorrow?"

"Only Guard knows."

"Where will the swallow take you?"

"To Guard."

"I can't wait to see you on a swallow." William was amazed at the image of a screaming swallow taking Great Aunt Daisy to Guard on its back. He couldn't begin to guess what it might all mean, but his elastic imagination was building a rich picture.

"We'll see." She closed her eyes as a wave of utter weariness swept over her. Images of Olav drifted through the clouds in her memory, handsome and youthful in his oiled yarn sweater and Merchant Navy duffel coat. The night they spent together in Glasgow, their lingering kiss and desperate embrace on the quayside at Greenock before he boarded the Norwegian freighter bound for Halifax. They had planned to marry on his return. She would never be held like that again. The telegram. The incomprehension, the denial, the desperate hope, the flash of hatred towards Germany, the abyss of a suddenly bereaved life.

In the far distance, she heard Geordie's quiet voice: "Come on, Willy, we'll let Daisy sleep. We'll come again another day."

The pock—pock—pock of tennis balls one cloudless August afternoon in Wadhurst, the rugged captain from the Scots Guards, bronzed and wiry from North Africa, limping, yet strong despite the deep scar down his left thigh. Whisky and soda, their insane passion on the pavilion floor, writhing on a collection of old cricket pads. Sleep drifted through her memory, enveloping her like smoke.

William could think of nothing else, announcing 10 times a day, "Daisy's going for a ride on a swallow. When can we go and see her again?"

Josie glanced at the wall calendar. "Daddy can take you over next Monday afternoon."

The anticipation of Monday Afternoon assumed gigantic proportions in William's life. He would watch his Daisy go for a ride on a swallow to Guard.

At Reception they were met by Nurse Eileen, who told Geordie tactfully that Daisy was 'very poorly' and that it might not be appropriate for William to go into her room.

"In what way is she poorly?"

"She became incoherent after breakfast and we put her to lie down. She's been in and out of sleep since then and shows no sign of moving. We're waiting for the doctor but the duty nurse thinks she might have taken a stroke."

Daisy's tiny crumpled form occupied a small part of the bed, her face looking towards the door, eyes open. She couldn't smile as her great nephew and his son entered. William ran over and hugged her. He evidently felt none of the revulsion that overwhelmed Geordie. However much he adored his great aunt he found it difficult to put his face against her waxy, yellowish, mummified skin.

"I thought you might like this." William fished in his pocket and pulled out a tiny carved wooden bear. His mother had recently brought it back from Berne. He had been inseparable from it for days. He put the bear in her hand; her fingers curled weakly over it. She tried to whisper but words wouldn't come out.

"The room's so stuffy. Shall I open a window Daisy? You might enjoy the fresh air." She remained immobile. Geordie eased down the top half of the sash window. A family of swallows was nesting in the eaves directly above the window and their excited screams filled the room. A faint smell of mown grass wafted into the room from the lawn below.

"Can you hear me, Daisy?"

She stared at him.

"Is there anything you want?"

She struggled to speak. A word came out. "Peace . . . " She held William's hand. He seemed to understand what was happening, with the instinctive empathy of the very young for the very old.

A swallow flew into the room through the open window. It circled close to the ceiling and came to rest on a picture rail. She was a young bird, with sleek satin-blue plumage culminating in a long forked tail. Geordie opened the window wider to let her out. Instead, another swallow flew in and circled the room, settling beside its companion. Daisy raised her hand weakly in the direction of the birds and mouthed indistinctly, "Olav. . . " The second bird circled the room again, found the open window and flew out. Daisy spoke almost inaudibly to the remaining swallow, waving feebly: "Go . . . off . . . go to . . . Olav . . . Shoo."

This swallow was more timid than her companion. She sat on the picture rail for a while before launching herself into the room, circling the ceiling repeatedly until she tired and returned to her perch. The bird's chest pounded from fear and exertion. William screeched excitedly as he watched the aerial drama. "Look at that bird, Daddy."

"Yes, Willy, that's a swallow."

"That's a swallow?" He cocked his head towards his father, his nose crinkling in disbelief. A swallow was something between a helicopter and a space ship, not a bird.

"Is that what's going to give Daisy a ride? How can she get on a bird?"

"I don't think she can. Maybe she meant something else."

Daisy lay still, her watery eyes focused on the trapped swallow. After a short time the bird launched off the rail, circled the room three times and flew out of the open window in pursuit of her companion. Daisy's eyes closed; an expression of serenity spread over her face.

"Is Daisy gone, Daddy? Did she fly away with the swallow?" He looked at the lifeless body, ran to the window and stared at the screeching swallows circling above the building.